"This is too important for either of us to let the past be a distraction."

Von settled back into her seat. She took Trinity's hand in hers to keep up the pretense of being his wife. His fingers were stiff at first, but it wasn't long before they closed around her hand.

Von swallowed back the emotion that rose into her throat.

Even after all this time, he tugged at her emotions. Just being near him...remembering. Despite the fact that she chastised him for remembering, she remembered.

All too well.

She wiggled her hand free of his.

This wasn't a good idea.

She remembered everything.

Von closed her eyes and cleared her head. She summoned the image of the person they were searching for and all other thought vanished.

Tonight—right now—nothing else mattered except finding that little girl.

DEBRA WEBB

COLBY BRASS

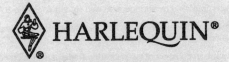

HARLEQUIN®

TORONTO • NEW YORK • LONDON
AMSTERDAM • PARIS • SYDNEY • HAMBURG
STOCKHOLM • ATHENS • TOKYO • MILAN • MADRID
PRAGUE • WARSAW • BUDAPEST • AUCKLAND

This book is dedicated to a man
I did not have the privilege of knowing personally.
But his reputation is one no one hereabouts
is likely to forget. Jerry Crabtree, a man
who did the thing he loved, police work,
until the day he died. Thank you, Jerry,
for a lifetime of commitment to serving
and protecting your fellow man.

Recycling programs
for this product may
not exist in your area.

ISBN-13: 978-0-373-69508-9

COLBY BRASS

www.eHarlequin.com

Printed in U.S.A.

ABOUT THE AUTHOR

Debra Webb wrote her first story at age nine and her first romance at thirteen. It wasn't until she spent three years working for the military behind the Iron Curtain and within the confining political walls of Berlin, Germany, that she realized her true calling. A five-year stint with NASA on the Space Shuttle Program reinforced her love of the endless possibilities within her grasp as a storyteller. A collision course between suspense and romance was set. Debra has been writing romantic suspense and action-packed romantic thrillers since. Visit her at www.DebraWebb.com or write to her at P.O. Box 4889, Huntsville, AL 35815.

Books by Debra Webb

CAST OF CHARACTERS

Evonne "Von" Cassidy—Von is a former Equalizer. She is focused and determined, but emotionally off-limits. She loved a man once, but refuses to admit that love still survives deep in her battered heart.

Trinity Barrett—Trinity is a protector. He will do anything to protect those he cares about. Can he save the woman he still loves?

Wanda Larkin—She has been seriously injured by her ex-husband, and her little girl, Lily, is missing.

Dennis Lane—He's a lowlife, but he's the one link they have to what Wanda Larkin's husband did with their daughter, Lily.

Waylon Robinson—He promises to cooperate. He knows where the children are...where Von is. But can he be trusted?

Special Agent George White—Simon's FBI contact, who has been investigating the human trafficking network spanning from Chicago to Alabama.

Victoria Colby-Camp—As head of the agency, Victoria sees only a bright future now that the Equalizers are fully merged with the Colby Agency.

Jim Colby—Jim wants his mother to be happy, no matter what it takes.

Simon Ruhl—A second-in-command at the Colby Agency. As a former special agent in the FBI, he has deep contacts with the Bureau.

Ian Michaels—As Victoria's other second-in-command, Ian is a stabilizing force within the staff.

Chapter One

Chicago, Tuesday, December 22, 2009, 2:05 p.m.

Only three days until Christmas.

Victoria Colby-Camp smiled as she watched the rush of last-minute shoppers along the sidewalks of Chicago's Miracle Mile.

Lunch with a longtime friend just two blocks from the office provided a nice stroll in the gently falling snow. Though many only endured Chicago's harsh winters, Victoria loved this time of year. It was filled with countless reasons to be joyous and to celebrate. Just six years ago she had celebrated her first Christmas with her son after more than twenty years of not knowing whether he was dead or alive.

Now she not only had her son, Jim, back, she also had gained a wonderful daughter, his wife Tasha, and two amazing grandchildren. A darling granddaughter, Jamie, and five-month-old Luke, Lucas James Colby. James would be so proud. The memory of her beloved late first husband brought a smile to Victoria's lips. He would very much approve of how far she and Jim had come despite the many obstacles life had thrown in their paths.

Victoria paused a moment to consider the building that had become home to the Colby Agency after the original building had been destroyed. Despite the state-of-the-art security, evil still found a way to touch those inside. Certainty chased away the niggling worry. No matter how hard their enemies fought to bring down the Colby Agency, somehow Victoria and her staff overcame the seemingly insurmountable to not only survive but also to thrive.

For this she was immensely thankful.

The chilly wind blew a wisp of hair against her cheek. Victoria swept it away, tucking the strands back into the French twist she'd so meticulously arranged that morning. Not so easy to do with gloved fingers. Sentimentality flowed inside her as she considered the numerous miracles she had observed firsthand over the past two-plus decades. The good somehow always outweighed the bad. She owed much to those who continued to persevere alongside her at the agency and fight the good fight.

Some had moved on to begin new lives elsewhere, but most remained invaluable assets, both as friends and as business contacts. The Colby staff was the best of the best. Victoria appreciated each one for his or her unique qualities. This year she and Jim had decided upon distinctly generous bonuses for every member of the staff.

Another smile spread across her lips. It was the

least she could do given the enormous sacrifices each had made through their continued dedication and loyalty during the ups and downs and changes with the agency.

A rush of pedestrians drew Victoria from her tender, affectionate musings.

"Did you see that?" a woman asked another as the two, headed in Victoria's direction, glanced back then hurried forward.

Victoria didn't hear the rest of the conversation since the women moved by so quickly. A group of pedestrians farther up the sidewalk drew her attention there.

A woman stood alone.

Victoria was first taken aback by her lack of suitable attire considering the freezing weather conditions. No coat...no hat or gloves. Dear God, no shoes. The woman stood, staring across the street, as if she expected someone or something to appear in her line of vision.

Then she turned, facing Victoria's direction, and trudged forward, her bare feet faltering clumsily through the ankle-deep snow.

Victoria's lips parted with a sharply indrawn breath.

The front of the woman's yellow blouse was stained a deep crimson. Droplets of that same startling color dripped from the fingertips of her right hand and onto the newly fallen snow, leaving a horrifying atlas of her jagged path.

Victoria's gloved hand slid into her coat pocket, wrapped around her cell phone even as a sort of shock held her unable to look away...unable to properly react. Who was this woman? What had happened to her?

She stumbled closer. "Can you help me?" Her lips were cracked from exposure and her skin was deathly pale from the icy cold.

Instinct kicking aside the shock, Victoria bolted forward just in time for the woman to collapse into her arms.

"Help me," she begged, her eyes wide with fear and glassy with whatever physical trauma she had suffered. Her left cheek was swollen. Blood had trickled from her nose and coagulated on her skin.

Victoria hit speed dial for the office as she lowered the woman onto the cold blanket of snow. "Mildred," she said before her personal assistant could launch into her practiced greeting, "I need paramedics. Now! I'm on the street in front of the office. I have a female, mid-to-late twenties, who is injured and bleeding."

Victoria surveyed the woman. The bleeding appeared to start at her left shoulder. "Make the call and get me some help out here!"

Tossing the cell phone aside, Victoria opened the bloody yellow blouse to assess the injury. A penetrating wound on the left shoulder. Deep. Still oozing precious blood.

"Please," the woman urged, her voice scarcely a gasp. "Help me."

"I've called for help," Victoria assured her as she shrugged off her coat and ripped the scarf from around her neck. With one hand she pressed the scarf over the wound to staunch the bleeding while spreading the coat over the woman's body with the other.

A sharply indrawn breath jerked Victoria's attention upward. A man, cell phone in hand, stared at the startling sight.

"Take off your coat," Victoria ordered him, "wrap it around her feet and legs."

Still frozen, the man blinked.

"Do it!" Victoria demanded.

His movements stilted, the man shouldered out of his heavy winter coat and moved to do as he had been instructed. "What…what happened?" he asked.

"I don't know," Victoria told him. "Help is on the way." To the woman whose lips were still moving with inaudible words, Victoria said, "Can you tell me your name?"

A weak gaze locked with Victoria's. "Help me," she murmured.

"You have my word," Victoria promised. "But I need your name." Sirens wailed in the distance, providing some amount of relief. Help was on the way. Thank God.

"My baby…" The rest of the woman's words were thready, indistinct whispers. "He took my Lily."

Victoria leaned closer. "Please, tell me your name." She wanted desperately to pursue the subject of the baby, Lily, but she needed the woman's name first.

"Wanda…" She moistened her cracked lips. "Larkin."

"What happened?" Victoria's son crouched on the other side of Wanda.

As if a shot of adrenaline had renewed her, Wanda Larkin frantically grabbed at Jim's shirt with her right hand. "He took my little girl," she cried. "You have to help me!"

Victoria's gaze collided with Jim's for an instant before returning to the woman's.

"Who took your baby?" Jim asked, his voice gentle.

"The paramedics as well as Chicago's finest are here."

Victoria glanced up at Trinity Barrett, a member of her staff. Like Jim, he hadn't taken the time to grab his coat before rushing out into the harsh weather. Victoria nodded, thankful the slippery streets hadn't slowed down the arrival of emergency services.

"Who took your baby?" Jim repeated a bit more firmly.

"My ex-husband," Wanda murmured. "He took my baby." Tears leaked from her glazed eyes. "I tried to stop him. Outside the toy…store." She gestured feebly in the direction from which she'd come.

As Trinity filled in the paramedics, Jim prompted more answers from the victim. Where did she live? What was the name of the toy store where the attack and abduction had taken place?

Victoria cleared her mind and took mental note of

the information Wanda managed to provide before her ability to listen and respond faded further. Victoria grabbed her phone from the snow and put through another call to Mildred with instructions to send Von Cassidy to the major toy store only a few blocks away. It was the only one in the direction Wanda had indicated. Every moment that passed lessened the likelihood of finding witnesses to the incident. There was no time to wait for the police to react.

Victoria and Jim moved aside as the paramedics took over care of the victim. While the police attempted to question Wanda, Jim gave Trinity a nod and they both slipped away. Victoria covered for them when the questioning turned to her and the man who'd reluctantly helped by giving up his coat.

By the time the paramedics had taken Wanda away in the waiting ambulance and the police had gone with a warning that there would likely be additional questions, Victoria was freezing. "Thank you," she said to the man whose name she couldn't immediately call to mind.

"I'm just sorry you had to ask for my help." He shook his head and offered a bewildered shrug. "You see these things on the news…in the movies…" He shook his head again. "But you never expect to be the one…"

"You reacted commendably," Victoria assured him before he trudged away. She surveyed the sidewalks where those who'd stood by watching now went on about the business of hurrying to their destinations.

When, she wondered, had helping one's fellow-man become more a spectator's sport than a call to action?

She peered at the bloody snow where the victim had lain, then up at the sky. Victoria closed her eyes and let the falling snow sting her cold cheeks. Who was this woman? This Wanda Larkin?

Was the incident related to a custody battle?

Or was this something far more sinister?

Either way...a child was missing.

Whatever the motive behind the act—Victoria shifted her gaze to the building where her staff waited—the Colby Agency would find the missing child.

And the man responsible for this unthinkable tragedy.

Chapter Two

Humboldt Park, 3:30 p.m. (2 hours missing)

Trinity Barrett surveyed the block surrounding the apartment building where Wanda Larkin lived. Jim Colby reached for the unsecured door leading into the building. Trinity followed his boss inside the dingy stairwell. The wails of an infant somewhere above the first floor were underscored by at least one blaring television. A woman shouting at someone who had evidently made her unhappy drowned out the rest of the cacophony.

Jim studied the row of mailboxes on the wall to the left of the entry door. "Third floor, 306."

Wanda Larkin had given them the street address, but the apartment number she'd murmured had been inaudible.

Three flights of stairs later, Trinity approached Larkin's apartment first. A metal number six identified the unit.

Jim held up a hand for Trinity to wait as he moved to the right side of the door and knocked loudly.

No response from the interior. No distinguishable sound.

Prompted by Jim's second round of knocking, somewhere on the fourth floor a dog barked.

Jim nodded his approval and Trinity reached for the doorknob.

Technically they were entering unlawfully, but the woman had given her address when Jim asked—which could be loosely construed as authorization to enter the premises. The cops hadn't arrived just yet, which meant Trinity and Jim would need to proceed with caution. Tampering with evidence could impede the investigation as well as get them in serious hot water with the authorities.

The latch released with nothing more than a single turn of the knob. Trinity pushed the door inward and drew back, staying to the left and clear of the opening.

Seconds ticked by with no reaction.

Jim moved into the doorway, then entered the apparently deserted apartment.

Trinity followed.

The place was neat and clean despite the worn-out furnishings.

No sign of a struggle.

The scent of recently baked cookies permeated the air. A small Christmas tree sat on the table in one corner, the decorations mostly homemade.

Jim headed for the small hall that likely led to the bedrooms and bath. Trinity moved around the living room. A couple of framed photos sat on a table in front of the window overlooking the unkempt street. No curtains, just the open slats of yellowed blinds.

Trinity picked up a photo of the woman, Wanda Larkin, and a small girl, six or seven years old, maybe. Cute kid with blond hair and brown eyes like her mother. His chest tightened at the idea that the child may have been harmed...or worse. He picked up another framed photo, this one probably taken at school. Her name, Lily, was stamped in gold lettering across the bottom of the photo. Using his cell phone, he snapped a close-up of the photo.

"Two bedrooms, one bath," Jim announced as he strode back into the room. "All are clean. If there's been any trouble here, there's no indication."

Trinity passed the framed photo of Lily to his boss. "I'll check the kitchen."

The kitchen was actually a part of the living room, the two spaces divided only by a breakfast bar. A plate of cookies decorated for Christmas sat on the counter. The little girl's artwork and more photos were displayed on the fridge.

Lily. Trinity touched the name scrawled on a pink piece of construction paper, then traced the cut-and-pasted Christmas tree the child had drawn. An innocent child...that was now in danger.

He shook off the troubling thoughts and focused on the details. Fridge and cabinets were painfully bare of provisions. Clearly the mother struggled financially, but the cleanliness of the apartment as well as the Christmas decorations and cookies indicated how hard she tried. A schedule printed on computer paper was taped to the side of the fridge. Trinity studied the document.

"She works at Mercy General," Trinity said aloud. The schedule gave no indication of the position she held, only the hours scheduled to work each day.

Jim joined him in the kitchen. "She scheduled to work today?"

Trinity shook his head. "Tomorrow afternoon." The numerous night shifts made him wonder who kept the girl, Lily, while her mother worked.

"I'm calling the police!"

Trinity and Jim turned simultaneously. An elderly woman waved a cordless phone receiver in her right hand while sporting what appeared to be a can of pepper spray in the left.

Jim's hands went up surrender style. "No need to call the police, ma'am," he assured her. "We're from the Colby Agency. We're here to help Ms. Larkin."

Trinity lifted his hands in the same fashion. "Are you a neighbor of Ms. Larkin's?"

The woman pursed her lips and narrowed her gaze. "If you're here to help her, why isn't she here, too?" she demanded, promptly ignoring Trinity's question. "Since she's not, that means you're here illegally."

Unfortunately, Trinity considered, the lady had a valid point.

"I'm Jim Colby," Jim explained, "and this is my

colleague Trinity Barrett." Jim gestured to his coat. "If you'll allow me, I'll gladly show you my ID."

The woman cocked her head. "Open that coat up so I can see if there's a gun under there."

Smart lady, Trinity decided.

Jim obliged, gingerly tugging open his coat using his thumbs and forefingers.

The woman nodded, a frizzy gray curl slipped loose from her haphazard ponytail. "You, too," she instructed Trinity.

Trinity did the same. Jacy Kelley, the agency's new receptionist, had appeared in the parking garage with Trinity and Jim's coats before they headed here.

"Come on over here where I can see." The neighbor wasn't stepping away from the open doorway.

Moving cautiously, Trinity and his boss again complied with her demand.

When they'd reached the center of the living room, she said, "That's close enough right there."

Both displayed their credentials.

After leaning forward to check out the IDs they offered, she eyed first Jim then Trinity with marginally less suspicion. "Where's Wanda and Lily?" Fury tightened her lips. "Has something happened?"

Jim explained the circumstances that brought them to Larkin's apartment, leaving out the part about the missing child. They needed this woman cooperative, not hysterical. Her face paled and her eyes widened at the few details Jim provided.

"I knew that no-good bum would do something

like this eventually." She shoved the canister of pepper spray into the pocket of her baggy jeans, shifted the phone to her left hand and extended her right toward Jim. "I'm Teresa Boles. I live cross the hall. I take care of Lily after school." As Jim shook her hand, she added, "He should've gone to jail for good the last time he knocked Wanda around."

"Ms. Boles," Trinity began as he, too, accepted a brisk handshake from the lady. Her grip was a heck of a lot stronger than he'd expected. "We'll need the ex-husband's name, phone number and address. Can you help us with that?"

"Kobi Larkin." Teresa wagged her head. "I haven't seen him in months. Not since he broke Wanda's jaw." She muttered a curse under her breath. "I helped her take out a restraining order and he hasn't been back. I hoped we'd seen the last of him." She suddenly frowned. "Wait." She looked from Jim to Trinity and back. "You said Wanda was at the hospital. Where's Lily?"

Trinity and Jim exchanged a look. "Ms. Boles," Jim said gently, "we don't know where Lily is. Bear in mind that Wanda was seriously injured and we can't be certain her story was accurate."

"Where's the baby?" Boles demanded, anger over-taking the fear in her voice. "Did that lowdown fool do something to Lily?"

"Ms. Larkin," Trinity took up where Jim had left off, "stated that her ex-husband had taken Lily. Do you have any idea where he might have taken her? Where he lives or works?"

"Why aren't the police doing something?" she shrieked. "There's no telling what he'll do! He's a dopehead! A no-good son of a bitch!"

"Ms. Boles," Trinity said coolly, hoping his rational tone would calm her, "the police are at the hospital with Wanda. They'll probably be here soon. We're trying to get a head start on finding the little girl. We promised Wanda we would find her. Anything you can do to help us will help Lily."

"We need as much information about him as you can provide," Jim reiterated.

She trembled, took a deep, shaky breath and squared her shoulders. "Kobi lives on the street, as far as I know. Don't have a job or a phone. But," she said when Jim would have interrupted, "the one thing I know for sure is that he hangs around with some other troublemakers over in Rogers Park." She shook her head. "I don't know any names of his friends," she added before Trinity could ask. "I heard Wanda say something about his friends in Rogers Park when she was yelling at him the last time he had the nerve to show up here. Before he broke her jaw. A couple of months ago."

"We'll check it out." Jim pulled a business card from his jacket pocket. "Ms. Boles, please call us if you think of anything else or hear anything related to Mr. Larkin or Lily."

Boles accepted the card, stared at it a long moment.

"What about the police?" She looked to Jim first, then to Trinity. "Won't they come here, too? Aren't you working with them? Do they understand that he's capable of anything? Just because he's Lily's father doesn't mean he'll take care of her."

"Yes, ma'am," Trinity answered, "the police will likely be here soon and have questions for you, as well. As we explained, we're trying to get a head start with locating the father so we can help Lily."

"Every second we waste," Jim said, his tone dull, emotionless, "may be the one that could have made the difference in how this turns out. You have my word that we'll do everything possible." He moved around the bewildered woman and headed for the door. "Call if you think of anything at all."

"Thank you, Ms. Boles." Trinity tried to reassure her with his eyes. "We'll find Lily." He started for the door.

"If it's not too late already," Ms. Boles called after him. "Kobi's crazy. He could do anything."

Trinity didn't slow his momentum.

Jim was right.

Every second counted.

Chapter Three

The police arrived at the toy store a full three minutes after Von, forcing her to adopt a different strategy for questioning employees.

In the past fifteen minutes they had taken four employees, one at a time, into the manager's office for questioning. Von couldn't eavesdrop so she had initiated her own approach.

First she'd visually examined the sidewalk and street in front of the toy store. No blood. Didn't make sense. The woman had been bleeding. Quite possibly her coat, assuming she had been wearing one at the time, had soaked up the initial blood lost. But where was her coat?

According to Victoria, the incident had taken place on the sidewalk in front of the store. Since the checkout counter and the restrooms were at the back of the store, it made sense to Von that any employee who'd witnessed the confrontation would have been working the aisles at the front of the store.

Von wandered the action figure aisle, the end closest to the two-story glass store front, and watched for the red apron the employees wore. The last-minute shoppers were out in full force. The thick crowd helped her to blend in. She glanced at the street beyond the heavily decorated wall of glass. Von doubted the two police cruisers parked out front were discouraging business since Christmas was just three days away. Some parents would walk over hot coals or dodge flying bullets to fulfill their kids' Christmas wishes.

Which was dumb in Von's opinion. Christmas was a waste of energy and resources.

A young guy, younger than her twenty-eight, rolled a float stacked high with boxes onto the aisle where Von waited. Depending on how long he'd been stocking these shelves he may have witnessed the confrontation between Larkin and her ex.

Half a dozen steps and she stood right behind the store clerk. "Excuse me."

He didn't turn around or acknowledge her presence.

She tapped him on the shoulder.

He jumped.

Then she saw the reason he hadn't heard her. His shoulder-length hair hid the wire extending from his ear to his MP3 player.

He snatched the earbud free and jammed it into his apron pocket. "Can I help you?" He cleared his throat. "I mean, sorry." He forced a smile. "How may I help you, ma'am?"

The distinct flicker of worry in his eyes warned that he'd committed this transgression before and wanted no part of that kind of trouble again.

"Have you been stocking on this aisle all afternoon?" Might as well get straight to the point.

He glanced past her, then searched her face a moment as if attempting to determine if she was a spy for management. "Since about one."

She hitched a thumb toward the front window. "My best friend had a big fight right outside with her ex. Did you see it happen?"

He stiffened. "I already talked to the police. I told 'em everything I know."

Von produced a trembling smile. "I can't get the police to tell me anything and I'm really worried. She's at the hospital and her ex took her little girl." Von shrugged. "I really want to find that bastard before he does something even more stupid."

The clerk licked his lips, checked both directions of the aisle. "I wish I could help you." He shrugged. "I really do. But I really did tell the cops all I know." He gestured to the floor to ceiling, wall to wall window. "I could see them arguing but I couldn't hear what they were saying. The dude grabbed the kid's hand and walked off. The woman ran after him. Looked like she was yelling but I couldn't hear what she was saying."

"Which way did they go?"

He pointed left and shrugged again. "That's all I know."

Von gave him a grateful smile. "Thanks."

The police would continue questioning employees until they were certain no one had seen or heard anything. Von had other plans.

If the violent part of the confrontation hadn't happened in front of the store, then it had to have occurred after the ex walked away with the kid in tow. Von moved out the front entrance and turned left.

Concentrating on the snowy sidewalk, she passed a restaurant, a bookstore and a pharmacy. When she reached the end of the block she turned around and retraced her steps.

No blood. Just the slush of snow beaten down by foot traffic.

How far had Larkin and her ex gone before the physical confrontation occurred? The Colby Agency was five blocks away. A street over and four blocks down. The woman had been bleeding profusely. Wherever she was attacked, presumably with a knife, there would be blood close by. If not on the sidewalk near the toy store...if not in front of witnesses who surely would have called the police— It had to be in a more secluded place. Some place no one would look on a busy afternoon only a few shopping days from Christmas.

Von checked the wide alley between the pharmacy and the bookstore. Some trash, a few empty boxes and a Dumpster but no blood. Double-checking as she retraced her steps, she returned to the sidewalk and moved on to the next possibility.

Between the restaurant and the toy store was another alley, this one too narrow for the city's garbage truck. Again there were empty boxes. A couple of garbage cans and not much else.

"Damn it." Had Wanda Larkin gotten disoriented and confused the location of the confrontation? Maybe she'd followed the jerk a considerable distance from the toy store.

Von ventured deeper into the alley. As she neared the end where the alley gave way to another sidewalk and street, her gaze snagged on a dark spot. Not mud or other grime. This was distinctly rusty in color. The snow was a slushy mess from the foot traffic but there was something...

She touched the spot, assessed the smudge on her fingertip.

Definitely blood.

Her heart rate accelerated as anticipation fired in her veins.

At the intersection of the alley and the parallel street that ran behind the toy store another stack of boxes were overturned and scattered.

More blood.

Von dragged box after box aside...a woman's coat had been wadded into a ball and tossed to the side. Von cautiously unrolled the coat. The lining was bloodstained. Fur-lined ankle boots were hidden behind more boxes...and socks—all bloodstained.

Judging by the amount of blood on the ground, Von estimated that Wanda Larkin had been immobile and hemorrhaging heavily for several minutes. Lying on the frigid ground with no coat and no shoes.

Fury roared through Von as she pieced together the story the elements of the scene revealed.

The ex had meant for Wanda to die.

Von sat back on her haunches and surveyed the scene once more. Larkin had stabbed his ex-wife or slashed at her with the knife. Von inspected the coat, noted the hole in the garment. Not an extended tear in the fabric, a distinct hole. No slash. He'd stabbed her. He'd hit her or pushed her hard enough to knock her unconscious or stun her, at least for a few minutes. Then he'd stripped off her coat and boots, tried to camouflage her body and walked away.

Leaving her to die.

Exposure to the extreme cold would have hastened the outcome.

"Bastard." Von pushed to her feet and double-timed it back to the toy store. She tracked down the guy she'd questioned before. "Do me a favor." The clerk didn't look too gung-ho, but Von went on, "Tell the police there's blood in the alley between this store and the restaurant next door."

The guy's eyes rounded. "Blood?"

"Tell them!" Von ordered as she backed down the aisle toward the exit. "Tell them *now*."

She didn't wait around to get caught up in questioning. Her SUV was in the parking garage down the block and across the street. On the way, she put in a call to Victoria and explained what she'd discovered near the toy store.

"Von, I want you to rendezvous with Jim and Trinity," Victoria instructed. "They're en route to Rogers Park. The ex-husband reportedly lives or spends time in the area."

"Do we have his name or a description?" Von asked, pushing aside the automatic reaction that had nothing to do with this case.

"His name is Kobi Larkin. Research is sending a DMV photo to your phones now. Also, Trinity obtained a photo of the child at the mother's apartment. He'll forward that to you as well." Victoria hesitated. "And, Von, tread cautiously," she warned. "Keep me posted. I'll follow up with Chicago PD."

"On my way," Von assured the chief of the Colby Agency as she sprinted to her SUV. Her mind raced ahead of her...to Rogers Park.

To *him*.

Trinity Barrett.

Living in the same city with him wasn't the end of the world. Not at all. Chicago was plenty big enough that running into each other wasn't exactly that big of an issue. He'd worked in the high-class section of the city; she'd worked on the fringes. Hadn't been a problem...until this year.

From the moment Jim Colby had told her the Equalizers were merging with the Colby Agency, Von had known this moment might come.

But she'd hoped.

She'd even prayed.

Well, sort of.

Now the nightmare she'd wished to avoid was becoming reality.

She would be forced to work with Trinity Barrett, her ex-husband.

After hitting the key fob and climbing into the driver's seat of her SUV, she jammed the key into the ignition and started the engine. She took a slow, deep breath and relaxed to the degree possible.

She could do this.

It wasn't the end of the world, Von reminded herself. Not really. Yes, it would be awkward and annoying and damned frustrating working with him. But there was every reason to anticipate that she would certainly survive the challenge.

He, however, might not.

Chapter Four

Rogers Park, 4:30 p.m. (3 hours missing)

Trinity waited at the corner of the block, the rendezvous point.

She was almost here.

Evonne Cassidy. *Von.* His ex-wife.

Trinity hiked his shoulders in an effort to relieve some of the stress. He should have resigned ten months ago when Victoria announced that the Equalizers were merging with the Colby Agency. But Trinity loved his work at the Colby Agency. He'd hoped that Von would do the right thing and decide not to come onboard at the agency.

But she'd done exactly the opposite.

Five years ago they had made the decision to end their volatile relationship. Problem was, neither of them had been willing to leave Chicago. Determined to make a fresh start Trinity had, in time, signed on with the Colby Agency. A couple years later he'd heard through mutual friends that Von had taken a position at another PI type firm, but he hadn't known until a few days later that it was Victoria Colby's son's firm.

That fact hadn't been a problem until this year.

Until then, Trinity and Von hadn't spoken since the divorce finalized, not for any reason. Shortly after the announced merger earlier this year, they'd had a face-to-face meeting in neutral territory. A decision to keep their history private had been reached. There had been no need to drag their tumultuous shared past into the present. They would be cordial to each other at work and if they were lucky, a mutual assignment wouldn't come up.

So much for luck.

He watched her SUV roll to a stop at the curb. This was it. No turning back.

They were professionals. They were both dedicated to their work. There was no time to deal with personal issues under the circumstances.

A child was in danger.

Von slid from behind the wheel, shoved the door shut with her hip and hit the key fob to initiate the vehicle's security system. Her trendy slacks and matching coat were signature Von. She liked being comfortable, but she never sacrificed fashion to make it happen. Somehow she always looked like she'd just stepped off a runway in the most casual of clothes.

Trinity swallowed hard as she marched toward him. He'd seen her every single weekday this year at the office. No matter, each time his internal reaction was the same—uncertainty, yearning…frustration.

Fool he was, even five years hadn't changed the way just watching her move made him feel. One thing was an absolute certainty, he would take that particular secret with him to his grave.

Giving her the satisfaction of knowing that she had the upper hand on his heart was one humiliation he had no desire to experience.

"Just received word from Simon that there are two possible addresses where Larkin has been known to hang out," she announced as she strode toward Trinity's position on the sidewalk.

Simon Ruhl was one of Victoria and Jim's seconds in command. Possessing deep connections within the FBI, Simon could generally reach out to his contacts for swift and relevant information.

"Excellent," Trinity acknowledged the news. It was a starting point. Rogers Park had more than its share of less than savory characters and locations. Wasting time sifting through them all was less than optimum under the circumstances.

Glancing past Trinity, then in the other direction, Von asked, "Where's Jim?"

Jim Colby was the former head of the Equalizers. It had taken time, but the crew who'd come onboard from the Equalizers and the staff at the Colby Agency had learned to consider both Jim and Victoria "the boss." Trinity doubted Von's question about Jim had anything to do with her considering him her *actual* boss. Most likely she had hoped a third party would be around to provide a buffer between the two of them. Trinity had hoped for the same. Just another example of how luck had deserted him completely today.

"He's on the phone with Chicago PD." Trinity pulled the collar of his coat up around his neck. "They're not too happy that we got the jump on their investigation. Larkin's neighbor mentioned we'd been in the apartment. Jim's doing damage control."

Von made a disapproving face. "That's ridiculous. Who cares who got the jump? Finding the kid is the goal here."

Her lack of patience with the rules was a leftover of Equalizer methodology. That tactic had slowly but surely been overcome in recent months. Von, like the others, had learned the Colby way of conducting an investigation. Granted, this situation called for swift, decisive action, still some amount of interfacing was necessary when boundaries were breached.

Enemies were easy to make. Allies were far more difficult to attain and even harder to keep. The Colby Agency prided itself on cultivating and maintaining strong allies.

"Where to first?" she prompted.

Trinity kicked aside the distractions and gestured to the apartment building to their right. "Kobi Larkin has a sister who lives on the second floor. The sister, according to neighbors, has refused to speak to him since he and Wanda divorced. We're hoping she can point us in the right direction."

"Larkin may be scum," Von commented as they

crossed the street, "but he's still the woman's brother." She shook her head as she surveyed both ends of the block once more. "In my experience a perp's family is rarely any real help so I wouldn't hold my breath."

Trinity couldn't cite any recent examples to dispute her assertion. But they had to try every avenue, no matter how remote.

Like the building where Wanda Larkin lived, this one was rundown and dingy. Despite the cold, four teenage males loitered on the steps leading to the front entrance. Von ignored their lewd comments. Trinity stared from one to the other, long enough to make them squirm. The door closed behind Von who hadn't hung around to watch his protective maneuver.

He caught up with her on the stairs leading to the second floor. She didn't bother glancing back. Von Cassidy could take care of herself and she didn't like anyone indicating otherwise—in word or deed.

Fixing his gaze someplace besides on her swaying hips was a task. Trinity was glad when they reached the second-floor corridor.

"Two-fifteen," he said as he led the way along the cluttered hall. Apparently tomorrow was trash pickup day. Most of the doors were flanked by bags of what had the look and smell of household garbage.

At apartment 215, he stopped and rapped on the door, careful to keep to the left in the event whoever was inside opted to take a shot at whoever had dared to knock. Von waited on the other side of the door.

"Who is it?"

The voice inside was female and distinctly unfriendly.

"Maggie Clemmons," Trinity began, "my name is Trinity Barrett. I'm an investigator looking into the disappearance of your brother, Kobi Larkin, and I have a few questions for you. I'd appreciate it if you'd open the door and cooperate."

Von arrowed him a look of approval. Nothing he'd said had been a flat-out lie, but he'd left out some relevant info like the fact that he wasn't a cop.

"I don't know anything about him or his friends," the woman claimed. "I haven't heard from that no-account bum in months."

"Ma'am," Trinity pressed, "just a few moments of your time will be greatly appreciated. This is a matter of the utmost importance."

Silence.

Von raised her eyebrows in question at Trinity.

He wasn't giving up just yet. "Ma'am?"

"I told you I don't know anything," came through the door.

"He took Lily," Trinity added since the concept that her brother was missing hadn't done the trick.

Trinity's gaze locked with Von's. If the child being in danger didn't get through to the woman…likely nothing would. Maybe Von had been right in her assessment. Blood was thicker than water.

Grinding metal echoed from turning locks, providing the response they had hoped for. Relief flared in Trinity's chest.

The door opened and a woman who'd obviously just saturated her hair with a color treatment looked from Trinity to Von and back. "He wouldn't have taken Lily." She shook her head adamantly as if that would make her words so. "No way."

"May we come in, ma'am?" Trinity didn't want to have this conversation in the corridor. Not with several doors cracked open just enough for nosy neighbors to see and hear too much already.

With a swipe to her brow with the towel dangling around her neck, the woman opened the door wider. "There's got to be a mistake."

Once Trinity and Von were inside, she closed the door. "Did Wanda say Kobi took Lily?"

"Ms. Clemmons, have you heard from your brother today?" Von asked.

Clemmons glared at Von, then blinked repeatedly. Apparently the pungent smell of the chemical hair treatment was getting to her. "I told you I haven't heard from Kobi in months." She blinked twice more. "Where's Wanda? Why didn't she come if what you're saying is so? She wouldn't just send somebody around saying such things."

"Wanda is at Mercy General," Trinity explained. "According to an update I received from my superior just a few minutes ago, she survived surgery and is currently in guarded condition." Victoria had called just before Von arrived. He probably should have mentioned that to her as well. But he'd been too busy worrying about how they would manage to work together without killing each other.

The woman hugged her arms around her waist. "He swore to me that he didn't hurt her. Is Wanda gonna be all right?"

So much for telling the truth.

"If Wanda pulls through with no permanent damage," Von answered the question, "she'll be very lucky. Kobi stabbed her, stripped her coat and boots off and left her to die in the snow beneath a stack of empty boxes in an alley where no one would find her."

"Dear God," Clemmons murmured.

"When did you speak to Kobi?" Trinity pressed, hoping to get the truth before Clemmons had time to rethink her position.

"About two o'clock, I guess." She dabbed at her forehead with the towel again. "He said they'd had a big fight, but that everything was gonna be okay. He said he was going away for a while. To get himself together." She turned her palms up in an earnest manner. "That's why he called. After all this time, he just wanted to say bye before he left." Her head wagged side to side. "He's pushed her around from time to time but he never hurt her…like this."

Not so according to the neighbor, but Trinity wasn't arguing the point. He needed this woman to keep talking.

"Did he give you any idea where he might be

planning to go?" Von demanded before Trinity could, keeping the pressure on.

Maggie Clemmons shrugged. "He just said he was owed some money and he was gonna use it to do the right thing...finally."

"Do you have reason to believe he planned to, as you say, get himself together?" Trinity hoped the man had perhaps gone into hiding with his child and meant no harm to her. Finding a scumbag like him wouldn't be that difficult. So far, he hadn't proven that smart. "To do the right thing?"

Clemmons heaved a weary sigh. "No. He's said that before. He probably took the money and got more drugs. That's what he usually does." She divided her attention between Trinity and Von. "That's why I know he wouldn't have taken Lily with him. He don't care about much but he does want her to have a better life. He's always said she deserves better than he or Wanda could give her."

"The fact of the matter is," Trinity said somberly, "he did take Lily, after leaving Wanda for dead. It doesn't sound like he has Lily's best interests at heart just now."

"We have to find him," Von added. "Before he allows any harm to come to the child...before the police find him. If you care about your brother you need to help us. You know what they do to people who hurt children."

Silence screamed in the room for two beats. Trinity hoped Von's strategy worked. A plea from woman to woman—one that included hope for the brother.

"Charlie Jones," Clemmons said with a confirming nod. "I don't know where he is. But Charlie knows Kobi better than anyone. He'll know how to find him."

"How do we find Charlie?" Trinity asked. "We have to hurry. There's no time for tracking him down. Not if you can give us that information."

Clemmons hurried over to the end table next to her sofa. She scribbled something on a pad of paper, then ripped the page free and brought it to Trinity. "This is his address. I don't know his phone number. But you'll find him here. If anyone knows where Kobi is, it's Charlie."

While Von thanked Ms. Clemmons, Trinity made his way into the corridor and put through a call to Simon Ruhl. By the time they reached the stairwell, Trinity had relayed the name and address to Simon for intelligence gathering. Any info available from any and all sources could prove useful in their approach.

Trinity dropped his cell phone into his jacket pocket. "Simon will call us if he finds anything." Since the address was only fifteen or so minutes away the preliminary info might be minimal, but they couldn't wait around for additional details.

Von put her hand out to push through the door of the building's front exit. "If we're—"

She abruptly whirled around. Shoved Trinity against the wall. And kissed him.

His fingers tightened in her coat with the intention of pushing her away...but they relaxed instantly as the reality that *Von* was kissing him sank into his brain. His eyes closed as the feel of her hot mouth moving over his trumped all other senses.

Vaguely he was aware that the door opened and people entered the building. He heard the shuffling of boots, the hushed exchange of male voices. Trinity wanted to open his eyes and assess the new arrivals but her tongue slid along his and all other thought vanished.

Her arms went around his neck and he promptly forgot the past five years...the hurt...the arguments... the loneliness he'd felt so many, many nights along with anyone or anything else he should have been thinking about just now.

"Get a room," a male voice grunted.

Male laughter faded along with the heavy footfalls tromping up the stairs.

Von suddenly drew away. "Let's go."

Trinity blinked. Grappled with the concept of what had just happened.

Von pushed out the door.

He swiped his still burning mouth with the back of his hand. "What the hell?" With a bewildered glance up the stairs, he shuffled out the door to catch up with her.

"You mind explaining what that was about?"

he demanded when he caught up with her hurried stride.

She jerked her head toward the street and the dark sedan illegally parked in a red zone. "Cops."

Trinity stopped. He stared at the sedan then back at the apartment building.

"Come on," Von called back. "We're wasting time."

Since Trinity had arrived in the neighborhood with Jim Colby, he didn't have much choice but to go wherever he went from here with Von.

He climbed into the passenger seat of her SUV.

His lips still tingled from the unexpected kiss.

It hadn't meant anything, he reminded that truly stupid part of himself that wanted to be psyched about the fact that she had kissed him for any reason.

Von would do whatever it took to get the job done.

Even kissing a guy she disliked...her ex-husband.

Trinity's cell phone vibrated. He pulled it from his pocket to check the screen. A text from Simon.

Proceed with extreme caution.

Target is dangerous.

More details to come.

Trinity confirmed that he had received the information. He slid his phone back into his jacket pocket and checked the weapon at his waist.

"Got your weapon?" he asked the driver.

Von sent him a sidelong glance. "Have you ever known me to be without it?"

An avalanche of memories twisted his gut.

At that moment Trinity wasn't so sure Charlie Jones was going to be the most dangerous aspect of this investigation.

He swallowed back the doubt.

Whatever he had to face…the top priority was finding that little girl and bringing her safely back to her mother.

Chapter Five

5:40 p.m. (four hours missing)

Von studied the photo of Charlie Jones sent via a multimedia message to her phone by Simon. Forty years of age, according to the stats accompanying the photo, long, stringy brown hair, cocaine-skinny with an extra long rap sheet. A real dirtbag.

Even worse, this was a friend of Lily Larkin's father—the man who had disappeared with her after stabbing and leaving her mother for dead.

Not good.

A snowman, leaning precariously to one side, adorned one of the postage-stamp-sized yards of rundown duplexes.

Only one streetlight worked and that was on the end opposite of where Von had opted to park, allowing for the possibility of trouble getting damned close without warning. The up side was that the dark provided good cover for her black SUV.

Lily Larkin had been missing approximately four

hours. Every additional moment that passed was one too many. Von wanted to find that little girl.

"The cops will be right behind us," Trinity commented. "If they get to Jones first, we'll be at an impasse."

"Then what're we waiting for?" Von had wanted to move as soon as they pulled to the curb. Her partner was the one who'd insisted they hold off.

Colby rules—the investigator with the most seniority at the agency was lead.

"That," Trinity said, his attention fixed on the row of housing "is what we waited for."

Two men exited the front door of the duplex suspected as being the hangout of Jones and his friends. The interior light disappeared as soon as the front door closed behind them but not before Von got a decent look at the man with long, stringy brown hair.

"He got a heads-up that the police are asking questions about him," Von said, voicing the realization that barged into her brain a few seconds later than it had her reluctant partner's.

"Can you stay on him without him noticing?" Trinity turned to her. "We can't risk losing him."

Von didn't justify his question with a response. She shook her head as she started the SUV's engine. They were married for three years, during which time she and Trinity had tracked down numerous bail jumpers as well as varied and sundry bad guys.

He knew her driving and surveillance abilities.

"Lots of things can change in five years," he noted as if that explained everything.

Another remark she wasn't going to bother rejoining.

She gave Jones a half a block head start before easing away from the curb. The sparse traffic made getting any closer dicey at best.

"He's taking the upcoming left."

Like she couldn't see the luxury silver SUV easing toward the center line. "Looks that way."

Von drove past the street the target had taken.

Trinity didn't say a word. He didn't have to. She felt his tension radiating across the center console. He would have chosen a different strategy. Tough, he wasn't driving.

She took the next left. Drove the short block and braked for the stop sign at the subsequent intersection. "And there he goes," she noted aloud as the silver SUV drove past their position.

Trinity said nothing as she made the right turn and followed the target.

Truth was, she couldn't read minds and the target could just as easily have gone in the opposite direction. That, too, would have been fine. She would have seen his taillights and followed. This neighborhood was pretty barren.

This street was flanked by rundown shops that had long ago closed for business. Scarcely any streetlights still worked. Jones was playing it safe, keeping a low profile in a deserted area where anyone watching was likely up to no good as well. And would be easily spotted.

Von's choice to take a different route had been a simple diversion tactic that had a fifty percent chance of success.

Brake lights abruptly lit the night as the SUV skidded to a sideways stop in the street.

Fifty percent chance of failure.

"Back up!"

Von had already hit the brakes and jammed the gearshift into Reverse before Trinity issued the order.

Something in her peripheral vision caused her to stall. She blinked as she watched the two men climbing out of the silver SUV. "They're running."

She hadn't realized she'd said the words out loud until Trinity bolted from the vehicle.

Von hissed a curse. The man was going to get himself shot jumping out in the middle of the street like this with two known scumbags already running scared.

She rammed the gearshift back into Drive and barreled around the SUV they'd left blocking the street, using the sidewalk for passage.

One of the men darted to the right into an alley.

Von braked. Her SUV slid to an abrupt stop and she jammed into Park.

Trinity overtook the man still running down the middle of the street.

Von released her seat belt and burst out of the

vehicle. She headed after the man who'd charged into the alley.

She reached beneath her jacket and wrapped her fingers around the butt of her weapon.

Her target body slammed a door in an attempt to break into the building to the right. The door didn't budge. He lunged forward once more.

Von was close enough to hear him panting for breath.

That was the thing about bad guys. They took lots of risks but didn't bother staying in shape.

She dove forward. Grabbed his jacket. Her momentum sent him stumbling forward, face-first onto the pavement. He tried to buck her off.

Clamping her thighs around his waist, Von shoved the muzzle of her weapon into the back of his skull. "Don't move." She grabbed a handful of stringy brown hair when his right hand continued to fumble around beneath him. "If that's a weapon you're going for, don't bother." She nudged his scalp a little harder with the business end of her .9 mm. He stilled.

"Slowly," she warned, "draw your hands from under you and spread them above your head." When he'd done as she instructed, she released his hair and reached beneath him. "No wonder you didn't pull it out sooner." His weapon had slid deep into his pants. For now, it was basically out of his reach, as well as hers.

"Charlie Jones?" she asked. Looked like him,

but it was pretty damned dark in this alley and she couldn't be certain.

"Who's asking?" he snarled.

She jabbed the muzzle deeper. "A friend." No wallet in his back pockets. She doubted he carried any ID. "Are you Charlie Jones?"

"Maybe. You a cop?"

"Look." She revised her strategy. "I'm not a cop. And I don't really care who you are or what you've done, I just want some answers about an associate of yours. Then you can be on your way."

Several seconds ticked off. "So ask. Maybe I'll answer."

Since she hadn't heard any gunfire she assumed Trinity's situation was under control.

"Kobi Larkin," Von said. "Where is he?"

The scumbag kissing the asphalt barked a laugh. "How the hell am I supposed to know?"

"You know him, right?"

"Yeah, yeah. So what? I know a lot of people."

Von twisted her fingers in the guy's hair and pulled hard. He grunted. "Did you see him today?"

"Depends," he snarled.

"Did you see him?"

"Yeah, I saw him."

She loosened her grip on his oily hair. "Did he have a little girl with him?"

The bastard snorted. "Yeah. Sweet little thing."

Von barely restrained the need to pull the trigger. "Where's the little girl now?"

The wail of sirens split the night air.

Jones or whoever the hell he was tensed.

"If you want a head start," she warned, "you'd better talk fast."

"He wanted to make some money," the lowlife said. "He had a *real* need, you know what I mean?"

Yeah, she knew exactly what he meant. "You gave him money? For what?" Fear and disgust exploded in her heart at the idea that any scumbag could be a parent. A person had to have a license to drive a vehicle...but anyone could be a parent—no prerequisites or licenses required.

"No. Man, I ain't into that." He made a disgusted sound. "But I know people...who are."

"Who did you send him to?" Damn it all to hell. This couldn't be right. What father would do this?

"Another associate of mine."

"What's his name and how do I find him?"

The sirens were closer now.

"I don't know his name. Just his phone number. I call him and he gives a drop location."

Von's stomach waded into knots. "You called him on your cell?"

"Yeah."

She reached into his pocket, pulled out the cell phone she'd felt when checking for his weapon. "Which number?" She opened up the log of recent calls, matched the one he recited from memory. A very close associate if he knew the number by heart.

Von pushed aside the personal feelings. She had to focus. The time the call was made seemed right based on the mother's statement of events.

"What do you get out of the deal?" Von couldn't keep the revulsion out of her voice, didn't even try.

"Twenty percent."

"Twenty percent of what?"

"A good-looking little girl like that? Thirty-five hundred. Sometimes more." He sniggered. "You'd think even an idiot would know that changing your mind isn't an option."

"What the hell are you talking about?" Von demanded.

"We're done," Jones growled. "Get off me before—"

Doors slammed on the street where she'd left her vehicle.

"Get off me!" He started to buck again.

She burrowed the muzzle deep into his flesh and leaned forward to whisper in his nasty ear. "Does he keep the kids or does he auction them?"

"He sells 'em," he muttered. "You said you'd give me a head start."

"I lied." Von pressed hard on his carotid artery. He tried to throw her off, but the insistent pressure won the battle, rendering him unconscious.

She rolled him onto his back and fished the weapon from his crotch.

A glance toward the street told her she hadn't been spotted just yet.

She sprinted in the opposite direction, tossing the bastard's weapon into a Dumpster. Having him wake up and use it on a cop or anyone else was a possibility she wanted to avoid.

At the other end of the alley, she checked the street in both directions. Another police cruiser, sirens flashing and blaring, skidded into a left turn headed for where her vehicle as well as Jones's had been left. Two Chicago PD cruisers were parked in front of the duplex reportedly rented or leased by Jones.

Von needed cover until she could determine Trinity's status and find new wheels.

First she had to get across the street without being spotted. Shouldn't be too difficult considering the lack of working lights along the block.

She skimmed the offerings along the block, the warm glow pouring from the windows of most proclaiming inhabitants. Likely armed and unfriendly.

Just pick one.

One, only one, was dark as if no one was home or it was vacant.

Von took a breath and headed across the street. She took her time. Strolled leisurely. Walked right up the steps of the porch. No chairs or benches available.

Her heart pounding, she sat down on the top step.

From the corner of her eye she confirmed that no uniforms had headed her way.

She sent a text to Trinity.

Status?

While she waited for a response, she sent a text to Simon Ruhl with the number Jones claimed was his contact for the sale of Lily Larkin.

Von's stomach cramped at the thought.

Don't think about it. Just do what has to be done.

Von needed an address…anything to reach this bastard. This trafficker.

Bile burned the back of her throat.

What're you doing sitting down?

Relief rushed through Von's veins as she read the text from Trinity. She glanced around.

I'm two houses to your right.

Von stood, walked across the porch, climbed over the rickety railing and jumped down to the side yard. She moved through the backyard of the properties until she reached the one where Trinity waited.

He leaned against the side of the house. "The police have Jones and his pal in custody."

"Did you get anything?"

Trinity nodded. "Jones brokered a deal for Larkin." He looked away. "He sold his daughter, Von." After a few seconds his gaze locked with hers once more. Even in the darkness she could see—maybe she felt—his simmering fury. "He sold her to get money for drugs."

She held up the cell phone she'd taken from Jones. "I've got his cell and the number he uses to make contact with this broker."

"We need a ride now," Trinity said as he checked his phone. "Jim's sending someone to pick us up."

Von's chest tightened. The child had been taken from her mother nearly five hours ago. She could be anywhere by now.

The screen of Trinity's phone lit with an incoming text.

They had to find this bastard. There was no time to wait for the police to Mirandize their suspects and attempt to get the information necessary to stop this travesty. The lowlifes would lawyer up and hours and hours would be wasted.

"This way." Trinity gestured to the row of houses behind them. "Two streets over. Jim's waiting."

Von hurried to keep up with Trinity's long strides. Her mind reeled with scenarios for locating this scumbag. Maybe Simon would have some luck with the cell number she'd passed along.

A dog barked.

Lunged at them.

Von jumped. She swallowed back her heart when she recognized that the dog was chained.

Trinity had her by the arm tugging her forward through the darkness between houses. Rectangles of light beamed through the windows, providing enough illumination for them to make their way through the maze of shrubs and trees. Her mind wouldn't stay focused on her steps. She could only think of the little girl.

Jim's sedan sat at the corner. He flashed his headlights to ensure they spotted him.

Someone else was in the front passenger seat. Trinity opened the back door and let Von get in first. Then he climbed in and closed the door.

"You two okay?" Jim asked.

Von nodded. Trinity responded, "Yes."

Simon Ruhl, the other passenger, shook his head. "Kobi Larkin is dead."

"What?" Von didn't understand. "How?"

"One of my contacts in Chicago PD," Simon explained, "let me know that Larkin's body was discovered in the duplex where Jones lives."

Von and Trinity exchanged a look.

"Wait." Von replayed her interrogation of Jones. "Jones said something like 'You'd think even an idiot would know that changing your mind isn't an option.'"

"Larkin changed his mind," Trinity concluded. "Jones or one of his associates killed him when he wouldn't let it go."

Von had no sympathy for the dirtbag. "Too bad he didn't grow a conscience until it was too late." How could the man sell his own child?

"The number you sent Simon," Jim said, "we're running it down now but it's not going to be easy. The person it belongs to doesn't want to be discovered via that means. It'll take time."

They didn't have time. "We have to do something now," Von argued.

"It may be too late already," Trinity reiterated. "These brokers work fast. She could be on her way anywhere by now."

"We're doing all we can," Simon offered. "Larkin is dead. Jones and his associate are in police custody. We'll move forward as soon as—"

Von turned to Trinity. "Call him."

"What?" Trinity's face scrunched in confusion.

"Tell him you have some merchandise," Von said quickly, the idea taking shape. "A fifteen-year-old female. You need to get rid of her today. Now."

Jim and Simon spoke up simultaneously. Both tossing out reasons her suggestion wouldn't work.

The confusion cleared from Trinity's face as if he'd just grasped the idea. "That kind of move would require bait."

"Absolutely," Von agreed, tuning out the arguments coming from the front seat.

Realization dawned in Trinity's eyes and his head moved side to side. "No way."

"It's the only way," Von argued. She glared from one man to the other. "There's no time. Waiting isn't an option and we all know it. We have to move now."

"What you're suggesting is out of the question," Trinity challenged.

"What's the big deal, Barrett?" Von demanded. She wasn't fifteen but that fact could be disguised long enough to get the ball rolling. "I've been bait before."

The silence that followed confirmed what she knew with complete certainty. All in the vehicle understood that her proposal was the fastest, most logical and effective way to move forward.

Setting up some sort of deal with the buyer was the only way to save this child.

Chapter Six

Mercy General Hospital, 7:30 p.m. (6 hours missing)

The rhythmic sound of the numerous machines hooked to Wanda Larkin kept the silence at bay. But nothing abated the underlying sense of worry and doom induced by the smell of the room. No matter the technology used, there simply was no way to make a hospital smell "inviting" or "comforting."

Victoria wished there was something more she could do for the poor woman she'd found on the street. Hours had passed since Wanda's lifesaving surgery and still she had not regained consciousness for more than a moment or so. The doctors and nurses assigned to her weren't overly concerned as of yet. With the mental as well as physical trauma she had suffered, it wasn't unusual for a patient to want to stay asleep. It was a defense mechanism.

Perhaps, since Victoria had no good news to report regarding Wanda's missing child, it was for the best.

Even now Victoria waited for an update from Jim or Simon.

A missing child, no matter the circumstances, was horrifying enough, but, dear God, at this time of the year when celebrating life and love were on the minds of most…it was unusually cruel.

A soft moan drew Victoria from her troubling thoughts. She stood and moved closer to the bed. Wanda moaned again, her head moving side to side ever so slightly.

Victoria took her hand. "You're in the hospital," she explained gently. "The doctors are taking very good care of you, Wanda."

The patient's eyes opened. She blinked twice then stared into Victoria's. "You have to help me."

Victoria patted her hand. "Everything that can be is being done, I promise."

Tears welled in Wanda's eyes. "He took Lily." She moistened her dry lips. "He took my baby."

"We know," Victoria assured her, her heart breaking with the idea that they hadn't found the child already. "We're retracing his steps in hopes of locating Lily."

"You're the woman…" Wanda's voice faded and she cleared her throat.

Victoria put a bendable straw into the cup of water from the bedside table and offered Wanda a drink. When she had dampened her throat, she squeezed Victoria's hand. "You're the woman who helped me. I remember…just you. No one else."

A smile tugged at Victoria's lips. "I'm Victoria Colby-Camp. Yes, I called for help and tried to keep you warm until help arrived. My investigators from the Colby Agency are looking for Lily right now."

Wanda's brow furrowed and her lips trembled. "He tried to kill me."

Victoria wanted to tell her that the bastard was dead, that he'd gotten what he deserved and none too soon. Kobi Larkin had died the same way he'd lived, savagely and ruthlessly. But, no matter how he'd hurt Wanda, he had still been her husband once and was the father of her child. Victoria wasn't sure she could deal with that truth right now.

"He tried to hurt you," Victoria agreed, "that is true. But you're going to be fine. You'll be up and out of here in just a few days."

Wanda tried to lever herself into a sitting position. "I have to find my baby."

Alarm trickled through Victoria. "You have to lie still, my dear. For now, there's nothing you can do." She ushered the patient back down onto the bed. "You won't be any good at all to Lily if you don't allow yourself to heal properly. Getting well needs to be your priority while *we* find Lily."

Wanda swiped at her tears with the hand not burdened with IV lines. "I can't just lie here while… he…" Her lips pinched with the fear widening her eyes, then quaked as she murmured, "I have to find her. He doesn't know how to love her like a father should."

"Following the doctor's orders is what you have to do," Victoria urged. "My agency and the police are doing all that can be done to find your daughter. There is nothing you could do even if you weren't stuck in this hospital bed. You must get well. Lily will need you when this is over."

"You swear?" she pleaded. "Swear to me that you'll find my baby."

Victoria knew better than to make a promise like that under any circumstances. There was no way to guarantee success, no matter how hard her people fought to make that happen. But the horror already haunting the poor woman's eyes tore at Victoria's resolve to maintain her professional boundaries.

"I swear," Victoria said, unable to hold back the promise. "We will find your daughter."

Chapter Seven

Warehouse District, 7:45 p.m.

Trinity had gotten his way.

It was a flat-out miracle.

Three years of marriage and never once had he won an argument with Von.

She wasn't happy about it, but she had thrown her hands up and given in. Rather than using Von as bait in a situation that could possibly have gone bad really fast, they had come up with a new plan that didn't involve bait at all. Rather, money was the sacrificial offering. Lots of money.

"If this guy doesn't show soon," she threatened, as if she'd read Trinity's mind, "we're going with the plan I suggested."

Trinity hunched his shoulders to draw the collar of his coat around his neck against the cold, then studied the dark street. "He'll show."

That was something Von would learn about the Colby Agency. If Simon Ruhl, Ian Michaels or Victoria Colby-Camp said it would be, then it would be.

This was a contact Simon had gotten from a former Bureau colleague—one Simon trusted. The contact would show.

This particular contact, a Dennis Lane, was not only connected to the Midwest human trafficking network, his number had also shown up on the downloaded list of calls to and from the number Charlie Jones claimed was his only means of contact with the buyer who'd purchased Lily Larkin. So far neither the agency nor the Bureau had been able to trace the number to a source, but Lane's number had popped out at Simon's Bureau colleague.

Now, Trinity and Von waited for Lane…hoping like hell he could make the connection to the dirtbag who had Lily.

Von folded her arms over her chest and leaned against the building. "Thirty minutes," she announced, her words a little muffled by the scarf wrapped around her shoulders and throat. "If he doesn't show in the next half hour, I'm out of here. I've got that junkie Charlie's contact number. I'm moving on it in thirty-one minutes."

Trinity didn't doubt her one little bit. Patience was not one of her virtues. Though she had a number of others. Not big as a minute. She stood a mere five-two and wouldn't weigh a hundred pounds soaking wet. But she wasn't afraid of anyone. His lips curled with amusement at the idea that an enemy might look at her and see a mere poodle facing off against a pit bull, but she rarely lost a battle, particularly one of wills.

She still kept her coal-black hair cut short. It hugged her face and neck in soft, silky wisps. And those eyes. Pure blue laser beams that could melt your heart or cut you in two. Her body was lean from plenty of cardio and well toned from pumping iron, but not so much so as to lessen the feminine qualities.

Those curves were firm and toned but, at the same time, soft and smooth. Not even five years had allowed him to forget.

"Are you finished?"

Trinity blinked, then quickly looked away. "I was just thinking." She'd caught him. Not good. And unfortunately it wasn't the first time.

"When are you going to stop doing that?" She pushed away from the wall and walked to the edge of the sidewalk to peer down the street, first one direction, then the other. She could never be still. "It's a waste of time," she added.

Anger instantly tangled in his gut. She did this every time. And he got ticked every single time. "Doing what?"

"Remembering." She sent that laser gaze in his direction. "The past is called the past for a reason. It's over. There's no going back."

"Oh, yeah." He shoved his hands into his pockets to prevent reaching out and shaking her. *"That."*

She wanted to pretend *they* never happened. Under

the ruse of moving on, she had tucked their three years of marriage into a tight little compartment and shoved it to the very back of her mind—never to be opened again. He hadn't been able to accomplish the feat. The memories were always with him…far too handy and completely unforgettable.

He couldn't move on. He was one hundred percent stuck in that past she proclaimed as over.

"Maybe that's our guy." She hitched her head to the right where a set of headlights bobbed as a dark sedan rolled over the potholed street.

Trinity resisted the urge to lean down and check the weapon in his ankle holster. No matter how dependable the contact, if he suspected trouble he wouldn't hesitate to protect himself from a perceived threat. Trinity tapped the communications device in his ear to ensure those listening understood that the target appeared to be approaching and the meet was going down.

Simon Ruhl and Jim Colby were parked in a nearby alley, monitoring the situation and providing intel as it became available. They would also provide any necessary backup.

The sedan eased to a stop in front of where they waited. The lack of working streetlamps prevented much in the way of visuals. The door opened, the momentary light from the interior allowed Trinity to visually confirm it was the expected contact.

"Barton?" the man asked.

Trinity nodded as he stepped forward. Myles Barton was his cover. "This is my wife, Louise."

Von, her arms still crossed over her chest, eyed the guy suspiciously. "I hope you aren't wasting our time, Mr. Lane. I don't like to be kept waiting."

"If memory serves," Lane said, his words directed at Von, "you called me, Mrs. Barton. Are you in the habit of calling on those you suspect incapable of accomplishing the goal?"

Von lifted her chin in that sassy manner that said she wasn't bested by the likes of this guy. "We'll see, won't we?"

Seemingly, unruffled, Lane shifted his attention to Trinity. "You're looking for a child in the three- to six-year range?"

"A girl," Von put in, taking a step in the direction of the men. "Blond hair," she looked to Trinity, "like her father."

Lane didn't like Von's pushiness; that much was obvious. But he also wasn't going to pass on the opportunity to make some extra cash. "These extra options can be expensive," he warned.

Fury tightened Trinity's gut. The bastard had just referred to a child as if it were an automobile. "I'm prepared to pay twenty for the child," Trinity pressed, careful to keep his disgust out of his face, "five extra for your trouble if you can make this happen in the next twenty-four hours."

Lane laughed. "Impossible. I'll need seventy-two

at the very least." He glanced at Von. "Especially if you're being picky."

"We're leaving for Texas on Friday morning," Trinity explained. "We haven't visited what's left of our families in seven years. We need the child with us. We want a minimum of twenty-four hours to orient the child…if you know what I mean."

Lane considered Trinity, then Von before shaking his head. "Your family believes you have a daughter?" He shook his head. "I don't even want to know."

"Good," Trinity cautioned, "because that's none of your business. Are we doing business or what? Time is wasting."

Lane shrugged. "Whatever. I've heard it all." His gaze narrowed then. "Seems strange that you waited till the last minute to do your *shopping*."

"You're our third contact," Von said with all the drama of a highly trained actress. "The others couldn't produce what we were looking for. I hope you're better than your competition."

Trinity's instincts went on alert. The guy's suspicion had mounted exponentially in the past minute. Pushing him any harder would have him backing out as surely as he'd just taken the step down from the curb putting him closer to his car.

"I might not be the right man for the job," he offered. "These transactions can be problematic. Frankly, overzealous buyers make me nervous."

Von's breath caught and her worried gaze landed on Trinity's. "You have to do something." She played extremely disappointed perfectly. "We're running out of time."

Trinity leveled his full attention on the man who had, for all intents and purposes, closed down his shop. "Fifty. I'm willing to go as high as fifty thousand for a girl and ten extra to you for making it happen *now*. Tonight with no further questions."

Lane hesitated only a second. "Sounds like you and your wife have a desperate situation."

"It's an inheritance thing," Trinity lied, "nothing you'd find interesting. But that's as high as I go," he warned when anticipation lit in Lane's eyes. "The time limit is nonnegotiable."

"Please, Myles." Von grabbed Trinity by the arm and played the part of the persistent and petulant wife. "She has to be blond."

Trinity could almost see the dollar signs flashing in Lane's expression. "Seventy-five. Total," he said flatly. "You bring me a little blond-haired girl meeting the right age criteria—tonight—and the money is yours. How you split it with your supplier is up to you."

"Brown eyes," Von piped up. She stared in feigned adoration at Trinity a moment before turning to the other man. "I want her to have blond hair and brown eyes. No substitutions."

The scumbag held up his hands. "I'll do what I can."

"If you can't do it," Trinity countered, "say so now. We'll move on to the next name on our list."

Lane's jaw hardened with something like anger. "I'll make it happen."

"When will we know?" Trinity pressed. "We have arrangements to make."

"I'll call you within the hour." Lane reached for the door of his vehicle, then hesitated. "Bring cash," he said with a blunt look at Trinity. "All of it."

"Cash," Trinity echoed. "Is there any other way to shop?" He gestured to his jacket. "May I?"

Another hesitation, then a nod.

Trinity pulled an envelope from an interior coat pocket and passed it to the man. "A little incentive to make up for the pressure we're no doubt causing."

Lane opened the envelope and fingered the cash. Five thousand in hundred dollar bills. He looked to Trinity with raised eyebrows. "You won't be disappointed." He got into the sedan and pulled away from the curb.

"He's suspicious," Von commented.

"He is," Trinity agreed. "But, I think his greed will override any lingering concerns he might have."

"It's cold."

She didn't look at him but he looked at her. He resisted the impulse to put his arm around her and pull her close, to warm her body with his.

But that would only make her angry.

"Let's go." He gestured for her to go ahead of him. "We can wait in the car or go to the coffee shop." The sedan they were using belonged to the Colby

Agency but was registered to a dummy corporation in the event the plates were run.

"I hate the waiting," she muttered as she reached for the door on the passenger side of the car.

"Yeah. Me, too."

That was the worst part of an investigation…the waiting. And the wondering. Was the little girl safe? Would they get to her in time? Would this elaborate ruse even accomplish their goal?

"Lane is making the call."

Trinity and Von's gazes locked as the words echoed through their communication links. Simon had just verified that Lane had made the call to the number Charlie Jones had insisted was the contact for the Lily Larkin buyer.

Trinity prayed they would get this lucky…that it would be this simple.

"Continue to the coffee house and wait for the call from Lane," Jim instructed via the com link. "We'll keep you advised."

Von acknowledged the instructions as she fastened her seatbelt.

Maggie's Coffee House was their destination. It was located directly across the street from the building that housed the Colby Agency. Simon and Jim would take up positions nearby as well.

The next few hours were far too crucial to leave anything to chance.

Von relaxed into her seat and remained uncharacteristically quiet during the drive across town. She usually had plenty to say, whatever the situation. Trinity started to make casual conversation but then the reality of the last few minutes hit him.

Von had made that remark about the past....

Trinity banged his head against the headrest. Simon would wonder about that, maybe even ask. When Trinity had come onboard at the agency that he'd been married before was in the background search. He hadn't attempted to hide it. There hadn't been any reason. Von hadn't hidden her past from Jim Colby—as if anyone could.

Their former marriage hadn't been relevant.

When the Equalizers had merged with the agency, new background checks hadn't been necessary for either staff. Jim's people had gone through rigorous security measures already as had the investigators at the agency.

Since Von had reclaimed her maiden name, evidently nothing had clicked. She and Trinity had opted to keep it that way. For better or worse.

This was something they would need to clear up when this investigation was over. Until now it hadn't felt relevant.

Trinity parked in the small lot on the Colby Agency side of the street.

"A meeting has been initiated with the Jones's contact," Jim advised via the com link.

Hope fired in Trinity's veins. "We'll be standing by." He wasn't sure where Simon and Jim would park. Possibly in the alley behind the coffee house.

Their sedan was nowhere in sight when he and Von emerged from theirs. Every precaution had to be taken to ensure this deal went down without a hitch.

"Careful," Trinity said as they crossed the street. Traffic was still fairly heavy with last-minute Christmas shoppers and the sidewalks remained treacherous with three days' worth of snow compacted and iced over in the less traveled areas.

Von marched across the street as if there wasn't a speck of snow or ice to be seen, much less traffic. Trinity took a bit more care. If he hadn't made the suggestion she would likely have moved more cautiously. She wasn't taking any orders or advice from him. He didn't know why he'd expected she would.

He supposed he deserved exactly the response he'd gotten. The break-up of their marriage was, to a large degree, his fault. He'd owned his mistakes. But nothing he'd said or done for a full year after the initial separation had changed her mind about the divorce.

Even after five years she hadn't forgiven him.

Maybe he hadn't forgiven her.

He moved ahead of her now to open the door to the coffee house. She indulged his need to play the gentleman, but she neither thanked him nor met his gaze.

It was too late to consider that working together on this case might be a mistake.

There was no going back.

"Coffee?" he asked.

"Definitely."

She didn't wait with him at the counter. Instead, she claimed a table away from the windows overlooking Chicago's famous Mag Mile.

He placed the order for two coffees. While he waited Jim and Simon entered and got in line behind him.

In the event anyone was watching, they didn't acknowledge Trinity or Von.

When Trinity had paid for the coffee, he walked past his colleagues without eye contact and joined Von at the table. He sat a steaming cup in front of her and took the seat across from her.

Trinity removed his coat and draped it over an empty chair. Before sipping his coffee he deactivated his com link.

As if she'd read his mind, Von did the same.

"There will be questions," he said.

"My mistake," she said.

Another first. Von rarely fessed up to mistakes. Then again, she rarely made them. She was very, very good at any endeavor she chose to undertake.

Good at a lot of things.

"I shouldn't have been staring," he admitted. It was true. If he hadn't been taking a trip down memory avenue she wouldn't have gotten annoyed…and the remark wouldn't have happened.

She leaned forward, braced her elbows on the

table. "This is too important for either of us to let the past be a distraction."

He nodded.

"I can hardly bear to think what that little girl might be going through." She closed her eyes and drew in a deep, steadying breath, then slowly released it.

Trinity couldn't help himself. He reached across the table and touched her hand. Her eyes opened instantly. "We'll get her back."

A small nod of agreement was her only response.

He knew what she was thinking, but he didn't dare say it. That would cross a line he wasn't prepared to risk crossing.

She blinked and the moment was over. As if he'd burned her with his hand she snatched hers away and straightened her back, putting as much distance between them as possible.

It was always the same.

There were things he wanted to say. But there was never a right time.

His cell phone vibrated.

He reached into his pocket and retrieved the phone, his gaze instantly settling on the screen. "It's Lane."

"I guess I misjudged him," Von said as she reactivated her com link.

Trinity slid the phone open. "Barton." He reactivated his own com link.

Lane provided an address in one of the city's suburbs. "Meet me there in one hour. Blond hair, brown eyes, six years old. She's ready to meet her new parents."

"We'll be there," Trinity assured him.

There was a moment's hesitation, then, "I checked you out, Barton."

Tension slid through Trinity. "I expected you would."

"Everything appears to be on the up-and-up," Lane allowed. "But, if you or your wife makes one wrong move. If I even get a whiff of a set-up, the deal is off. You got it?"

"Got it."

"One hour," Lane echoed.

"We'll be there," Trinity confirmed. He closed the phone and slid it into his pocket.

"We set?" Von's face reflected the worry she'd picked up on in his.

"All set." He glanced toward the table where Simon and Jim waited. Trinity repeated the address as much for Von's sake as for Jim and Simon's. "Anything feels wrong to him and the deal is off."

Von pushed her chair from the table and stood. "We'll just have to make sure nothing feels wrong."

Which meant backup would have to stay way, way back.

Just in case.

Chapter Eight

St. Patrick's Church, 9:33 p.m. (8 hours missing)

Just beyond Chicago's business district St. Patrick's Church stood tall and proud in the darkness. The two spires, as different as day and night, towered forbiddingly over the street.

St. Patrick's was the second oldest church in the city, one of the few structures to survive The Great Chicago Fire. Architecturally it was admirable, but Von had never been much of a churchgoer.

It had something to do with God abandoning her when she needed Him most. She let it go the first time it happened, when she was thirteen. But then... six years ago, He let her down again.

The past was the past, she reminded herself.

She shivered, though they sat in the relative comfort of the car. Just staring at the hulking structure of the church with the snow falling around it felt foreboding somehow. The holiday decorations were another sore spot with her.

Face it, girl, you have some serious baggage.

Trinity, of all people, should see that.

Whatever. This investigation had to be her total focus right now.

That they were to meet Lane—a man who profited from the sale of humans—was likely the underlying factor motivating her feeling as she'd been cast into some sort of sinister theater production.

The briefcase containing the money and two state-of-the-art tracking devices was in the backseat. Backup was stationed two blocks away, well outside possible enemy detection range. Von had strapped a .32 to her ankle, as had Trinity. Communication links were in place. Backup, Simon and Jim, would be aware of every word.

Once again Lane was running a few minutes behind.

Trinity reached into his jacket and withdrew his cell phone. He glanced at the screen, then at her. "It's Lane." After pressing the necessary buttons, Trinity said, "You're late. We had a deal, Lane."

The hesitation that crackled in the air warned that Lane understood he was on speaker.

"I have you on speaker," Trinity put in quickly, "my wife is here, *waiting,* with me."

"I'm very disappointed, Mr. Lane," Von managed to say though her mind still reeled with the idea that Trinity had called her his *wife.*

That was her role in this undercover operation.

She was Louise Barton, wife to Myles Barton.

But it felt...strange.

"There's been a change of plans."

An alarm wailed in the back of Von's brain.

"I'm paying you exceedingly well, Lane," Trinity reminded their contact. "You came highly recommended. I have no patience for games. You should have given me a straight up no before you took my money. This conversation is over."

"All is in order, Mr. Barton," Lane hastened to say. "We've changed the transaction location. That's all. I have what you want."

Trinity held Von's gaze. "I'm not happy about this, Lane." Trinity allowed a beat of thick silence. "But I'm prepared to move forward."

"Just one more thing," Lane said.

"Mr. Lane, this is becoming tedious."

Von's attention flew to the rearview mirror to the glare of headlights approaching from their rear. She clutched Trinity's sleeve and nodded to the rearview mirror. Three seconds later a gray sedan pulled up next to theirs. The dark tint on the windows concealed the driver as well as any passengers.

"I'm sure you understand what you need to do," Lane said.

"Lane—"

"This is ridiculous," Von snapped, cutting Trinity off. "We're supposed to get in this gray car you've sent and just go wherever it takes us?"

Lane had severed the telephone connection.

Von's door opened.

Her gaze collided first with the business end of a

weapon. "Get out," the masked man holding the gun demanded.

Behind her, Trinity was receiving a similar order.

"There's no need for guns," Trinity said. "I don't know what's—"

"Do as you're told and shut up," the man holding the weapon aimed at Trinity commanded.

Von climbed out, as did Trinity. Their escorts led them around to the gray sedan and ushered them into the backseat. Trinity's escort snatched the cell phone from his hand; Von's ripped the purse from hers.

After a quick search of her purse, he held out his hand. "I'll need your cell."

Von dragged the phone from her jacket pocket and placed it in his hand. "I just got that phone," she complained with the petulance that was a trait of her cover. And any info she could give to Jim and Simon via the com link, the better.

"Get in," the man roared, pushing her toward the open door of the gray sedan's back seat.

When she and Trinity were inside and the doors closed, the man who'd ushered her into the car dropped into the front passenger seat. He settled the briefcase containing the money in the seat between him and the driver. The tracking devices inside would ensure Jim and Simon were able to follow their movements despite the abrupt change in plans.

As soon as the doors closed, the sedan peeled away.

"Where are you taking us?" Trinity demanded. "What's going on here?"

"You'll have your answers soon," the guy in the passenger seat said with a glance toward Trinity.

Von settled back into her seat. She took Trinity's hand in hers to keep up the pretense of being his wife—who would unquestionably be frightened at the moment.

His fingers were stiff at first, but it wasn't long before they closed around her hand.

Von swallowed back the emotion that rose into her throat.

If he would just let it go.

Even after all this time, *he* tugged at her emotions. Just being near him...remembering. Despite the fact that she chastised him for remembering, she remembered.

All too well.

She wiggled her hand free of his.

This wasn't a good idea.

She remembered everything.

Von closed her eyes and cleared her head. She summoned the image of Lily Larkin and all other thought vanished.

Tonight...right now...nothing else mattered except finding that little girl.

They were headed away from the city.

Von's instincts bumped into hyperspeed. She didn't dare look back to see if backup could be spotted somewhere in the distance.

Jim and Simon were too good to be given the slip by these morons. She glared at the two masked men in the front seat. And there were the tracking devices. She and Trinity were covered. Not to mention they were both still armed, but playing this out in an attempt to get as much information as possible was necessary.

It was possible that their contact had opted to take extreme measures to ensure security, but Von had been in this business too long to hold out more than a fleeting hope on that score.

Lane had been suspicious all along.

The prospect of a highly lucrative deal had kept him from walking away...but, evidently, someone higher up the food chain had made him see the hastiness of his decision and made the final call.

There would be no deal tonight.

More likely she and Trinity would be taken somewhere and interrogated. It wouldn't be pretty. And, unless, backup intervened, they wouldn't likely survive. Lane would get the money either way.

Funny, she considered Trinity's profile, she'd started out in this business with him. He'd had that swagger down to a science. The cowboy boots and the worn soft jeans. He'd charmed her with one look. But that had been a long time ago. Now, after all they had survived, it looked as if they would be ending their careers together.

But it wouldn't be without a fight.

She crossed her legs, placed her right hand on her

knee, allowed her fingers to slip down to her ankle and trace the outline of the weapon strapped there.

As if his gaze had summoned her, she turned to the man at her side. His lips tilted upward just a fraction…just enough for her to know that he wasn't worried.

He wasn't going down without a fight, either.

Her heart bumped hard against her chest when his hand closed around hers once more.

They would get through this.

It wouldn't change things between them but at least they would be alive.

HALF AN HOUR OF SILENCE elapsed before they reached their destination.

The driver parked in front of a barnlike structure. Beyond the small clearing the area around the structure was wooded. The moonlight reflecting off the snow gave the place an eerie look. Two SUVs were parked to one side.

The men in front climbed out.

"Don't do anything until I say so," Trinity murmured to her a split second before their doors were wrenched open.

She nodded her understanding.

Not wanting to be dragged from the vehicle, Von emerged and started forward. The muzzle of her escort's handgun jammed into her back as a reminder that she should continue her submissive behavior.

Two SUVs were parked outside the building.

As they approached what she now realized was in fact a barn, the wide doors opened.

Inside was nothing at all like a barn. No stalls. No hayloft. There were concrete floors and fluorescent lights. Desks and chairs and two sofas. Several doors lined the far end of the structure. All were closed. No windows.

A transfer station.

Considering the goods Lane traded in and the out of the way location...definitely a transfer station.

This was where they brought the kids...where they kept them until they were shipped out.

Disgust twisted in her stomach.

There were four more men inside. None wore masks. All looked like average, run of the mill working guys. The two who'd escorted them here at gunpoint removed their masks.

Bad sign.

Any time the enemy didn't care if you saw their faces was bad.

It meant they weren't worried about their hostages giving away their descriptions or identities.

The hostages were going to be in no position to give away anything.

They would be dead.

Damn.

Von scanned the faces. Lane's wasn't among the group. Three were thirtysomethings, late twenties maybe, and appeared physically fit. The fourth was older and heavier with a bit of a bulge hanging over his belt.

"Put 'em in three for now," the guy with the bulge ordered.

None of the doors on the back side of the structure were visibly numbered. One of the men who'd brought them here hustled them toward the third door from the left. Von tried to get a closer look at the layout of the larger room, a command center obviously. A couple of computers. Her escort pushed her forward.

"Did you ensure they weren't armed?" the bulge guy asked.

Well damn. Then again, they'd been lucky to get this far without the subject coming up.

The surprise on their escort's face gave the answer to the man who'd asked. "Why would they be armed?"

Give the guy a "stupid criminal" award. Lane might have been suspicious but this guy clearly had swallowed the bait, hook, line and sinker.

"Do it," his chubby pal ordered. "Now." As if to reiterate his words, he strode up to Trinity and patted him down.

The dummy they'd come to this dance with, did the same to her.

The older guy shook his head as he stared at Trinity's .32. "Mr. Lane is not going to be happy about this."

"Self-protection," Trinity said pointedly. "I don't

go anywhere without it. Any man who does is a fool."

Their gazes held a moment longer, but the older guy didn't say anything in response.

Once they were shoved into room three, the door was slammed shut and they were left to wait for the next move. Unarmed and with a dead com link. Trinity had discreetly tapped his link several times with no response. Something was wrong with the link.

But they still had the hidden tracking devices in the briefcase.

Von wanted to rail about the deal going back to Trinity but he held a finger to his lips. He was right. The room could be and probably was bugged.

There was no furniture in the room. Not a single chair or a table. Only a plastic box filled with toys. She walked over and picked up a fuzzy bear. This was a holding facility, all right.

Lane hadn't just been suspicious, he had known. He wouldn't have brought a customer to a holding facility. He had known they were undercover operatives of some sort before he'd made the call tonight.

Now he would want to know who had hired them and what exactly they knew.

The money was irrelevant.

It was insured and marked for tracking purposes. Unless it was skillfully laundered first, anyone who tried to use it would be caught.

Von hoped she got to witness that part.

The door opened.

She and Trinity turned to face whatever came next.

A man rolled a utility cart into the room.

A second man carried two folding chairs. He placed them in the center of the room. "Sit," he ordered.

"Where is Lane?" Trinity demanded, keeping with his cover. "We had a deal."

"We won't need him for this," the man with the cart explained. He gestured to the chairs. "Have a seat."

"This has gone far enough," Trinity protested. "I demand that you take my wife and I back to our car. You clearly do not understand who you're dealing with."

"You're right," the one at the cart said as he picked up a roll of duct tape. "That's what we're going to find out."

"What's he talking about, Myles?" Von asked, feigning fear, which wasn't that difficult.

"It's all right." Trinity hugged her. "We'll get through this."

"Sit," the man who'd delivered the chairs roared yet again.

Trinity waited until Von had taken her seat and then settled into his. Their hands were taped behind them. Their ankles were bound and then a strip of tape was placed over their mouths.

How creative.

The men left the room.

If there was anything else on the cart besides duct

tape and what looked like a rope, she couldn't see it. Maybe the whole thing had been a scare tactic designed to get them primed for talking.

Von had already spotted two cameras. They were being watched. Any attempts they made to free themselves would be futile.

There was one thing she could do. Maybe their captors would even expect her to do it.

She bounced up and down in her chair, scooting it closer to Trinity. When she'd gotten close enough she placed her head on his shoulder and blinked rapidly as if holding back tears.

He smelled good. The same sexy scent he'd always worn. It reminded her of other scents and sensations. Like salty sea air and the spray of the ocean's wild, crashing waves. If she closed her eyes she could conjure up the feel of sand between her toes...and the wind on her face. They'd taken their honeymoon in the Bahamas. Warm, beautiful...the most amazing week of her life.

Too bad it hadn't lasted.

The door suddenly opened and two men entered once more.

Lane was one of them.

Von felt the tension in Trinity's posture.

Lane turned to his colleague. "Bring the woman first." He glanced at Von before walking out.

Trinity struggled with his bindings as the man approached her.

The man manacled her arm and jerked her to her feet. "Let's see how long it takes you to talk."

Since she couldn't exactly walk with her ankles taped together he pitched her over his shoulder and started for the door.

Trinity broke the folding chair getting out of it, but then fell face-first onto the floor.

There was nothing he could do.

The door slammed shut, cutting him off from her view.

The bastard carrying her hefted her into another chair, this one in the main space of the building.

Lane stared at her for a long moment, then said, "Start with the toes. If she doesn't talk, move to the fingers. I want to know exactly who they are."

Von had two options. She could just tell the truth, spill the beans, right up front and die quickly. Or she could attempt to hold out, maybe come up with something that would keep both her and Trinity alive.

The tape was ripped from her lips. She winced.

"Do you want to talk now?" the man in charge of her interrogation asked. "Or." He cut loose the tape around her ankles. "Lose a little toe?"

"We have money," she offered with all the uncertainty and fear she could muster. "A lot more than what's in the briefcase." That should give them something to think about.

The guy braced a hand on each arm of the chair and leaned in, putting his face close to hers. "You trying to buy time, lady?"

"Just trying to save us both some time," Von explained. "My husband and I are in a time crunch of our own. We need that little girl."

The bastard trailed a finger down her cheek.

She drew away from his touch.

"How much money?" he asked as he traced that same finger down her throat.

She resisted the urge to kick him in the crotch. He was in the perfect position. And he had cut the tape on her ankles. But she would play it this way for a bit and see what happened.

"Maybe three times that much at my husband's office in a safe. Even more in the bank." If she was going to lie, she might as well make it good. Not only did she not have a safe in her little apartment, she also felt reasonably certain Trinity didn't, either. Not unless his rich uncle had died since they divorced.

Then again, she was relatively certain he didn't have a rich uncle.

"Let's see what the boss has to say about that." The man straightened away from her. "Lane!"

Lane looked up from his cell phone conversation and held up a hand indicating he needed a moment or two.

While they waited, Von surveyed the movements of the others on site. She had counted four men besides their two escorts when they'd arrived. Six, altogether. Lane made seven. All were accounted for except two as far as she could see. She stretched her neck and considered the four doors across the back of the building. Number three from the left was where Trinity was. That left three other rooms. Were there prisoners in those rooms? Abducted children? Maybe Lily Larkin?

Wait...if there were cameras in the room where she and Trinity were held, surely there were monitors out here somewhere. Maybe she could get a glimpse of who or what was in the other three rooms.

She saw no monitors displaying scenes or spaces like the room she had been in. One computer screen displayed a map. Making out the details of the map was impossible from where she sat. The other computer screen was also a map, this one constantly moving like a weather map.

How were these dimwits monitoring the cameras in the rooms? Then she knew. Unless these guys carried some sort of personal, handheld monitoring systems, the cameras were nothing more than inoperable visual deterrents.

She couldn't be absolutely certain but it was a strong possibility. Good to know in the event she survived the next few minutes. Testing her theory wouldn't be that difficult.

Lane finished his call and strode over to where she and her would-be interrogator waited.

"She says there's three times what's in the briefcase at her husband's office in a safe."

Lane eyed her speculatively. "I don't believe you and your husband are who you say you are. Why would I believe this?"

Von remembered to look and sound afraid. "We just want a little girl. We have some very important business to take care of in Texas. It's about money. And…" She looked away. "I want a child."

Lane snickered. "You really expect me to believe that if we let you go right now, with a kid to call your own, that you'll forget this whole thing happened?"

Von blinked several times for effect. "My husband will lose his inheritance if we don't show." Before Lane could interrupt, she added, "Two million dollars."

Now both bastards appeared interested.

"Tax free," she went on, "But there has to be an heir for him to collect. It's one of his crazy grandfather's stipulations. He has to be married and have an heir. We've been traveling extensively the past few years. We haven't been home. Mainly because my husband and his father had a falling out. Anyway, we claimed there was a child. A little girl. We've never sent pictures. Never really talked about her. The estrangement made it easy to pull off." She leveled her gaze on Lane's. "But that's all changed now. His grandfather is dying. We have to have that little girl."

Lane continued to analyze her a few moments more, then he said to his pal, "Bring the husband to me."

Von hoped she had bought them some time.

The man returned with Trinity whose hands and mouth were still secured with the tape.

"You and I," Lane announced, "are going to pick up something from your safe at home." He gestured to Von. "Your lovely wife will wait here for our return. Need I remind you that her continued well-being will be solely dependent upon your complete cooperation and satisfying results?"

Lane ripped the tape from Trinity's mouth and stuck it to his shirtfront. Unlike Von, Trinity didn't wince. He glared at the man.

"What did you do?" Trinity demanded of Von as if furious with her.

Although they had a cover and had gone over the details she had just passed along to Lane, confirmation was necessary.

"I told them about the money in the safe," she explained. "And—" she swallowed as if nervous "—exactly what's at stake."

Trinity shook his head, then arrowed a furious gaze at Lane. "We had a deal. You reneged on that deal. And now you want more money?"

Lane shrugged. "Only if you want your wife to remain breathing. We'll get the money, return here, and you and your wife will be free to go."

"What about the child?" Von demanded. "The little girl?"

Lane gave another of those nonchalant shrugs. "You can have her." He smiled at Von, then at Trinity. "We had a deal, after all."

He was lying. She and Trinity would be dead as soon as the possibility of making any more money was off the table. This bastard had never intended to do business with them. Simon's contact didn't know this guy nearly as well as he'd thought.

"Mr. Barton and I will be back," Lane said to the others in the room. "Be prepared to move out as scheduled." He gestured for the man who'd driven them here to follow him.

Trinity glanced back at her as Lane ushered him toward the door.

He was worried.

Von couldn't say she wasn't.

But at least one of them was out of here.

Trinity would take care of Lane and his henchman. She'd just given Trinity his ticket out of here.

Von surveyed the room and the five other men milling around. All she had to do was create her own exodus, though there wasn't a single window and the only exterior door she'd confirmed was the one they had entered. There would be a way. All she had to do was find it and then she was out of here.

But not until she knew who or what was in those other rooms.

If there was even one child in this building, she wasn't leaving without him or her.

What she needed was an opportunity.

She couldn't wait for opportunity to knock.

"Excuse me," she announced to the room at large, "I need to use the restroom."

It was a ploy as old as time, but it was a tried-and-true one.

One of the men glanced at the escort who'd brought her here. "You take care of her. We have final preparations to make."

She was hoisted up and dragged to one of the doors at the back of the room, the second from the left. The goon opened the door and gestured for her to go in.

It was a bathroom, two stalls, one sink.

She turned her back to the guy and wiggled her hands. "You'll have to cut me loose."

With a heavy sigh, he cut her hands loose and then pushed her toward the door. "Make it fast."

Von shut the door in his face and quickly did her business. The request had been a ploy, but she wasn't going to pass up the opportunity to relieve herself. Before flushing the toilet, she pressed her ear to the wall that separated this room from the first room. She closed her eyes and listened hard.

Nothing.

Wait…a whimper?

Then she heard it clearly.

Crying.

Whoever was in the first room from the left was crying.

Sounded like a child.

Fury whipped through Von.

That solidified her determination. She wasn't leaving here without the child…or children.

Chapter Nine

"There must be security or traffic cameras some-where in the nearby vicinity," Jim argued with Simon's Bureau contact who was present via the tele-conferencing system. "St. Patrick's is barely outside the downtown business district."

Simon and Victoria sat at the conference table in her office. But Jim couldn't sit. Von and Trinity were out there...somewhere. Their sedan had been found on Adams Street near St. Patrick's church. At the rendezvous location. Jim and Simon had been a mere two blocks away. The moment communications were severed they had moved to the rendezvous location.

Only to find an empty sedan, front doors standing open.

The last verbal exchange captured by the com-munications link was of Von demanding to know where they were going.

Jim and Simon had determined that the vehicle to which Von and Trinity were transferred had been equipped with jamming devices, disabling the communications link as well as the tracking devices in the briefcase as soon as the doors were closed.

Damn it!

Simon had touched base with his contact for any additional information and support. At this point their only hope was to pick up via security or traffic cams the gray sedan leaving the area of the church.

It was a long shot, but it was the only one they had.

George White, Simon's contact, had been more than patient. Jim recognized that he had about half an hour ago crossed the line of reason.

"There are a number of cameras in the downtown area," White agreed, "but no silver or grayish sedan was picked on any of them between the time you heard the exchange and you arrived to discover your investigators' deserted vehicle. These men were obviously versed in the streets and blocks to avoid."

The telephone on Victoria's desk buzzed. She hurried to answer it.

"White, this contact of yours can't be pressured into revealing any details he perhaps has held back regarding this Lane character?"

"He insists he knows nothing more," White explained via the speakers of the conference table's teleconferencing system. "He can't name Lane's buyers or his contacts in the trafficking world. Lane once worked in the drug smuggling business with my contact. He moved on, it seems, to a different kind of cargo. My investigation into this human trafficking network is just getting its legs. We have a long ways to go."

Jim shook his head. This was getting them nowhere.

"Mr. White." Victoria had returned to the head of the conference table. "Please let us know if you learn anything at all that might be useful to our investigation. We appreciate your assistance."

White assured Victoria that he would and the call ended.

"What's going on?" Jim asked his mother. White was the only contact to Lane they had. Cutting off communications with him for the moment had to mean there had been a significant development.

"That was security," Victoria said, her voice quivering just a bit. "Trinity Barrett is on his way up in the elevator."

Jim didn't bother asking how that was possible. Victoria, Simon and he rushed into the corridor and on to the reception area to await the elevator's arrival.

A soft chime announced the car's stop on their floor, then the doors slid apart.

Trinity stepped forward. "I don't have much time."

Chapter Ten

"Lane and one of his men are waiting in the car in the alley less than a block from here," Trinity explained. He hated this part. He needed to get what he'd come for and get out of here...get back to Von. "I have five minutes to exit the building."

"Where is Von?" Jim Colby demanded.

Trinity swiped a hand over his face. He felt numb. Leaving her had been one of the hardest things he'd ever done. "She's at the transfer facility—or what appears to be a transfer facility. She's okay for now. The facility is about thirty minutes south of the city. We didn't take 94 and I'm not completely certain I can find my way back. The dark window tinting prevented me from monitoring the road signs. I'll need Lane to get me there."

"Why did he bring you here?" Simon asked.

"Money," Trinity said flatly. "To buy time, Von told them that we had more money at my office. I think she's attempting to persuade Lane that our quest to get a child is real and that we don't care how much it costs or what they're doing."

"You understand," Victoria said in that calm tone that spoke of unending strength and hard-earned wisdom, "that you're beyond that point now. Whatever else you and Von do, this man intends to kill you both."

Trinity nodded. "I know. Right now I need weapons I can conceal from these bastards and I need money." He reached inside his jacket and peeled the duct tape off his shirt. "This has Lane's prints on it."

Simon carefully accepted the tape. "I'll bag this and have it processed."

"I'll take care of the weapons," Jim said. "Come with me."

Victoria nodded. "Simon and I will prepare the money for transport."

Trinity inhaled his first deep breath since leaving Von in the hands of those bastards. He followed Jim down the corridor to the supply room. Trinity had no idea how much money the agency kept in the safe, but it would have to do.

Jim pressed his thumb to the scanner on the massive walk-in safe that was the arms room and then entered the pass code. The door opened and he and Trinity entered.

The arms room was a new addition to the Colby Agency offices. It had been added in the rebuild after the original offices were destroyed a few years back. In Victoria's office, a smaller version was camouflaged behind a paneled wall. Money and other negotiable assets were kept there. Swift and decisive action was only accomplished when fully prepared for most any scenario.

"Not even the smallest handgun we have will work," Jim said as he surveyed the offerings.

"I'm well versed in the use of knives," Trinity reminded him.

Jim selected a lightweight but lethal-looking switchblade. He passed it to Trinity. "Open the lining of your interior jacket pocket and drop the knife into the bulk between the lining and the leather."

Trinity used the knife to slit the pocket's lining, then carefully burrowed the knife in the material inside. "Done."

Jim gestured to Trinity's left wrist. "Take off your watch."

Trinity removed the watch and accepted the one Jim handed him.

Jim tapped the crystal face of the watch. "Crush it against your opponent's throat. A small dose of tranquilizer will be injected into the skin when the crystal breaks. He'll be out for the better part of an hour."

With the watch on his wrist, Trinity waited for the next tool.

A silver pen. "Press the top down as if you're preparing to use the pen for writing, then jab it into your opponent. This tranquilizer will put an elephant down."

"That'll work." Trinity placed the pen in his right jacket side pocket.

"Let's see if Simon and Victoria have the money ready to go."

They moved back toward Victoria's office, but Trinity hesitated before entering. "I told Lane my office was on the third floor. He can't see the front of the building from the alley, but I don't want to risk that he or his pal might be watching from another vantage point." A large wall of windows in Victoria's office overlooked the street. With the lights on, movement could be spotted from the street.

"Of course." Jim went to the door and asked his mother and Simon to join them in the corridor.

"There's one hundred thousand in here," Simon confirmed as he passed the portfolio type case to Trinity. "That's all we have readily available."

It wouldn't be enough, but it could work until he had subdued the enemy. He grasped the leather handle of the case in his right hand.

"Negotiate," Jim suggested. "Tell Lane you'll give him more once Von and the child he promised are with you and safely away from the place you were held." Jim handed him a tiny round disk. "Place this anywhere on the exterior of the car, it's magnetic, and we'll be able to track you. We couldn't track you before because there appeared to be a jamming device in the sedan that transported you from Adams Street to the transfer facility. Putting this one outside should alleviate that concern."

Trinity had presumed as much. He kept the small disk in his left hand. "Lane is smart," Trinity related. "Don't get too close." And that was assuming Trinity got the opportunity to place the device at all. "If I make any calls or summon help in any detectable manner, Von dies."

"There are security cameras all along the Mag Mile," Simon advised. "Whatever happens with the tracking device, we can capture your movements for some distance in that manner."

Victoria followed Trinity back to the elevator while Jim and Simon hurried down the stairwell to reach the basement garage and their vehicle in hopes of tracking Trinity's departure with Lane.

"Be careful," Victoria urged.

Trinity nodded then pressed the button for the lobby.

Her worried gaze remained on him until he was in the elevator and the doors slid closed.

Trinity squeezed his eyes shut as the car moved downward. He sent a silent plea heavenward that he could do whatever necessary to ensure Von's safety.

She had given him this shot at freedom. He had to make it count.

"Night, Mr. Barrett," the security guard called to his back as Trinity hurried across the lobby.

Trinity hesitated, then walked back to the security desk. He reached across the desk and tapped the notepad on the counter. "Make a note that I won't be in the rest of the week," he said. "In case anyone asks."

The bewildered guard nodded. "Yes, sir."

"Thank you." Trinity turned and headed for the exit. Inside, where the security guard couldn't see, he was shaking.

He couldn't let Von down.

Once before he'd done that and he'd lost her.

He couldn't let that happen again. Losing her had been bad enough, but letting her die...no way.

As HE'D SUSPECTED Lane met him on the sidewalk before Trinity reached the alley.

"I thought you said your office was on the third floor. I didn't see any lights go on."

"My office is an interior one," Trinity explained. "You wouldn't have seen the light. I didn't bother turning one on in the reception area."

"What's on the fourth floor?" Lane asked, suspicious as usual.

"More offices," Trinity said, allowing his frustration and impatience to show. "Accounting, I believe. But I've never been up there so I really don't know."

"Their lights were on," Lane countered. "I saw at least one person pass a window up there."

"It's almost the end of the year," Trinity tossed back at him. "They're likely preparing for tax season. Who knows?"

That seemed to satisfy Lane for the moment. "Give me the bag."

Trinity passed him the portfolio. Its weight made the bastard smile.

"You know the way," Lane said, gesturing for him to go first.

When they reached the alley, the sedan's engine revved to life but the headlights remained dark.

"Let's see what's in the case," Lane suggested. He motioned to his colleague who got out of the vehicle. "Pat him down," Lane ordered his driver.

Trinity held his hands away from his sides to facilitate the man's pat down, then held his breath, again praying that the guy wouldn't find the knife or the pen. He would need both when the time came.

Lane placed the case on the hood of the car and opened it. It wouldn't take him long to see that there was only a hundred thou inside.

The guy doing the pat down found the pen and shoved it into his own jacket pocket. Trinity noted that it was in his left pocket.

Thankfully the scumbag didn't notice the knife. Trinity had been wearing a watch previously so he didn't pay any attention to that.

"There's only a hundred thou here," Lane said, anger simmering in his tone. "Your wife indicated there was a lot more than this."

Time to play the tough guy. "That's right," Trinity said. "We go get my wife and the child you promised us and I'll give you another hundred thousand. I'm no fool, Lane. You've already double-crossed me once tonight."

Lane's associate slammed Trinity against the wall of the building behind him. "You're in no position to dictate conditions. We want it now."

Trinity shook his head. "Not until you hold up your end of the bargain."

"Kill him," Lane ordered.

Trinity laughed. "That would be a mistake."

Lane stormed up to him and shoved the muzzle of a weapon into his face. "How do you figure that, smart guy? You don't seem to have any advantage at the moment. They'll find your body in the snow tomorrow morning. Just another holiday mugging. People get desperate around the holidays."

"I left a note with the security guard. If anything happens to me, they're to look for you, Lane." Trinity grinned. "I provided a very detailed description and your fingerprints."

Lane's gaze narrowed. "You're lying."

"You didn't see me talk to the security guard." Lane had been watching. Trinity knew he had.

"You couldn't have left my prints," Lane argued.

"The duct tape," Trinity reminded him. "You ripped it off my mouth and shoved it on my shirt. I've seen it on television a thousand times. Can you be certain your prints aren't salvageable from the tape? All I want is my wife back and the child you promised us. Why would I contact the police then?

Buying children is a crime, isn't it? I have no desire to go to jail."

"Put him in the car," Lane roared. He strode back to the car, grabbed the portfolio and climbed into the front passenger seat.

"You think you're pretty smart, don't you?" the scumbag still holding Trinity against the brick wall jeered.

Trinity shook his head. "Just desperate, that's all."

The bastard pulled Trinity away from the wall and slammed him into the car. The tracking disk flew from his hand. There was no opportunity to see where it landed before the bastard shoved Trinity into the backseat.

Well, there went any chance of Jim and Simon tracking the vehicle.

Trinity wasn't going to sweat whether he had backup or not for the moment. He was prepared to take control of the situation and then he would contact backup.

Right now he needed to watch what he could see of the passing landscape through the front windshield and when he felt confident that he was close enough to find his way back to Von's location he would make his move.

He could handle the current odds. Back at the transfer facility his chances were less than optimal.

He studied Lane. Greedy bastard. That greed and

Von's quick thinking were the only reasons either of them was still alive.

That was the thing about bad guys. Even when they were smart enough and ballsy enough to pull off near-perfect crimes, their greed or need for power always got them in the end.

Lane's would get him.

Twenty minutes into the ride Trinity recognized the deer crossing sign they passed on the long stretch of deserted road. Someone had painted a red *X* on the sign. One of the few landmarks he'd been able to note. They were close. Eight or ten minutes, no more.

"We need to pull over." Trinity clamped his hand over his mouth.

Lane twisted around to glare at him. "What's the problem?"

"I'm…" Trinity grabbed at the door latch. "I'm ill," he muttered.

"Don't move," Lane growled and aimed his weapon into the backseat.

Ignoring the threat, Trinity released the lock on his door and pulled at the handle. Cold air rushed in around the partially open door.

"Shut that door!" Lane shouted.

The driver swerved as he attempted to determine what was going on in the back seat.

Trinity opened the door a little farther. "Can't…" He heaved, making it as authentic as possible.

"Pull over," Lane instructed the driver.

The car braked hard and rolled to a stop onto the shoulder of the road.

Trinity rammed his upper body out the door and made more sounds of having to empty his stomach.

Lane jerked Trinity's door open. Trinity scrambled out of the car and moved on all fours into the darkness. He kept up the fake heaving and groaning.

"What the hell's wrong with him?" the driver demanded as he came up alongside Lane.

"Who knows?"

Trinity mentally prepared a plan, then slowed the gagging and groaning.

"Get him back in the car," Lane ordered his subordinate.

Trinity braced.

The driver stalked over, reached down and grabbed Trinity by the left arm and hauled him to his feet. "Let's go."

A car door slammed, indicating Lane had already climbed back inside.

Trinity shook loose from the guy's hold and bent down to brace his hands on his thighs as if he might be sick again.

The driver opened the back passenger side door and came back to usher Trinity inside, grabbing him by the arm once more.

Trinity rammed the back of his free hand and wrist into the guy's throat, crushing the watch crystal with the impact. The guy let go of Trinity and stumbled back. He reached for his throat with one hand and his weapon with the other.

Lane was out of the car before Trinity could go for the knife in the lining of his coat or go after the special pen the other guy had shoved into his own pocket.

Trinity shoved upward the barrel of the weapon that leveled in his direction. He threw his full body weight into Lane, pinning him against the car.

Lane headbutted him. Shoved him backward. They tumbled to the ground where the other guy lay crumpled and unmoving.

Trinity fought to gain control of the weapon. Lane wasn't letting go. They rolled, alternately gaining and then losing the upper hand.

One shot, then two and three expelled from the weapon Lane attempted to turn toward Trinity. Fighting equally hard to keep the muzzle away from his person, Trinity finally got Lane on his back and began to beat the hand clasped around the butt of the weapon against the pavement. Somehow they'd managed to roll right up next to the front bumper of the car.

Two more shots fired off. Trinity dared to shift his attention to the guy's head. He slammed it into the pavement instead of the weapon. He slammed it hard, then harder.

The grip on the weapon loosened.

Trinity drew back his fist and punched him in the

jaw. Lane's eyes lolled back in his head. He stopped struggling.

Taking a second to catch his breath, Trinity pulled the weapon from Lane's slack fingers and shoved it into his waistband. He pushed to his feet and staggered over to the other guy to retrieve his weapon as well as the tranquillizer pen.

He made his way to the driver's side of the car and got the keys. When he'd opened the trunk he loaded Lane, and then his buddy inside. Trinity shot a couple of holes into the raised lid of the trunk just in case. He didn't want the bastards to suffocate. Even if they deserved no better.

Lane's cell phone wasn't in any of his pockets. The other guy's was but the keypad was locked. Trinity threw the phone into the woods, snagged the guy's weapon, then shut the trunk lid.

Stretching his neck after the rolling around on the ground, he made his way to the driver's seat and dropped into it. He shoved the key into the ignition and gave it a twist.

Nothing happened.

Not a sound.

He tried again.

Still nothing.

Trinity exhaled a frustrated breath. He pulled the hood release and then got out.

Nothing appeared to be wrong under the hood.

Then the engine should start.

A bad feeling niggling in the back of his brain,

Trinity walked around to the side of the car where the scuffling had taken place.

Most of the rounds that had gotten pulled off from Lane's handgun had gone into the side of the vehicle between the wheel and the passenger compartment.

Trinity shook his head.

He didn't know what one or more of the bullets could have hit and it had to be a one in a thousand possibility, but something about the vehicle's electrical system had apparently been damaged.

The engine would not turn over. The interior lights wouldn't come on. No heat. No radio. Nothing.

Trinity searched for Lane's cell phone, starting with the first place they'd fallen to the cold, frozen grass. After a minutes' frustration, he found it on the ground a few feet from the car.

"Blast it!" He tried a number of different combinations to unlock the keypad. None worked. The fifth attempt disabled the phone entirely.

"Perfect." He tossed it deep into the woods as well.

Trinity stared down the dark, desolate road. He knew the way from here. But it was quite a distance when measured in steps. He'd just have to run it. If he was lucky there would be a house along the way.

If he was even luckier Simon and Jim would pick up their route on one or more of the city's traffic cams and maybe, just maybe they would come in this direction.

Until then, he was on his own.

On foot.

Chapter Eleven

Wednesday, December 23rd, 12:01 a.m.

Von rubbed her hip and stared at the ceiling.

She'd almost made it that time.

But that worthless folding chair kept *folding* at just the wrong moment and throwing her off balance.

"One more time."

The guys in the other room surely had heard her bumping around in here but no one had come to see what she was doing.

Maybe they didn't care as long as they knew she was in here and more money was on the way.

Whatever.

She'd pushed the metal cart against the wall, then braced one of the folding chairs beneath its wheels to ensure it didn't roll away. The second chair she'd stacked on top of the cart to give her the height she needed to reach the drop-style ceiling. This close to the wall the support system would be well braced and she should be able to move a tile aside and climb up there.

Her goal was to move across the ceiling and see what was in the room to her right. The bathroom was to her left. No point looking there first.

The cart had more duct tape and rope and nothing else. She'd wrapped a length of rope around her waist in case she needed it and pocketed a roll of duct tape. Then she'd taped the heck out of the chair in hopes of preventing it from folding.

She climbed onto the cart. Took a breath and stepped up onto the seat of the rickety chair.

She could reach the tile directly over her head with her hands and had successfully pushed it out of the way the last go around. But pulling herself up there was proving the difficulty.

Her gloves had so far prevented the metal of the brace work from cutting into her palms. She grabbed on and closed her eyes.

Pull.

Her arms shook with exhaustion from the previous three attempts.

"Don't give up. Don't give up," she murmured.

Be strong! Pull!

Her head and shoulders rose above the brace work. She dared to release her hold with her left hand and swing her arm over the support beam.

Take a breath.

Relax a second.

She was halfway there.

It was dark as pitch up there. She let go with her right hand and wrapped that arm around the broad support beam that ran atop the wall that separated her room from the next one.

If she could get up onto the beam, she could slide a tile away on the other side of the dividing wall just enough to see who or what was in there.

She leaned forward with her upper torso, snaked her right leg upward. Getting her leg and booted foot through the opening and swung up onto the beam was a major hurdle...but she made it.

With a little more effort she was lying facedown along the length of the beam.

Lights were on in the neighboring room. She reached down and lifted the corner of the nearest acoustic ceiling tile.

Slowly...don't make a sound.

The room appeared to be empty...at least what she could see of it.

She leaned her head down. Dared to raise the tile a little higher.

Something darted across the room.

Von blinked.

What the...?

She lifted the tile higher still.

Her heart stumbled.

Six children, all small girls, huddled against the wall farthest from her.

Dear God.

Tiny gasps echoed in the room.

Six sets of eyes were suddenly focused on the ceiling.

Von hadn't realized she'd said the words out loud.

She managed to get a finger to her lips in the universal gesture for quiet.

With effort she slid the tile completely aside, leaving an opening about eighteen inches by thirty-six inches, the same as the one she'd climbed up through. The only difference was there wouldn't be a chair or cart on this side of the wall for her to drop down onto.

Couldn't be helped.

She had to get down there.

Holding her breath and fighting her quivering muscles, she eased one leg, then the other over the edge of the beam and through the opening.

She hung onto the beam with both arms wrapped around it.

Next she had to ease downward until she was holding on with nothing but her fingers.

From there it would be a four foot or so drop.

Good thing she hadn't worn high heels.

"Who are you?"

The gasp she heard then was her own. She took a breath, told her pulse rate to slow. "My name is Von. I'm here to help you."

Lots of whispering and moving about below her.

Von tried to see what was going on, but all she could see was the children gathered somewhere beneath her.

"You need to move so I can drop down," she whispered as loudly as she dared.

More whispering and a couple of groans.

"Here." Something touched Von's foot.

As best she could tell the children had made a support bridge of sorts and were attempting to help her down.

"I might hurt you," Von argued softly. "You should move."

"Just let go," a small voice urged.

Von held her breath and forced her fingers to release from the steel beam.

She slid down the wall.

Literally.

Little hands and bodies kept her pressed against the wall so she landed upright and on her feet.

Other than a stinging cheek, she was okay.

When she turned around, six small girls were huddled a few feet away, wide eyes staring at her.

"Did the police send you?" the girl who looked to be the oldest, maybe ten, asked.

"No," another whispered gruffly. "God sent her, silly."

Von held her finger to her lips once more, then hurried over to the door to listen. The men were talking, arguing maybe. She couldn't make out the words, but they were definitely having a fierce discussion.

She turned and surveyed the room that was all white and square just exactly as hers had been only without the cart and folding chairs.

How the heck was she going to get these kids out of here?

She moved toward the huddle of girls. Terror lit in their eyes.

"Are there others here?"

"See," a little red-haired girl grumbled, "she's not an angel. If she was she'd know that."

Her status had just dropped several notches. "We don't have time to talk about that now. Just tell me how many others are here."

The oldest stepped forward. "I saw six others."

Twelve. For Pete's sake. "Are you all okay?" She surveyed the small faces. "I mean, are you hurt in any way? Cut? Bruised? Bleeding?"

Heads wagged side to side.

"Good." Von moistened her lips. "What about the others?"

"One little girl was crying a lot," the oldest said.

"Way more than the rest of us," the redhead added.

Could be scared. Could be hurt. "You didn't see any injury? No blood or anything?"

Heads wagged in unison once more.

"Okay." What next? "What're your names?"

"Tara," said the oldest.

"April." The redhead.

They went down the line from there. Janey had blond hair. Katie, brown. Sophie had coal-black hair. And Lydia had brown corkscrew curls. They ranged in age from seven to ten.

All lived in Chicago or nearby towns.

There were a lot of questions Von would have liked to ask, but she had to focus on finding a way out.

Maybe if she could get them up into the ceiling cavity, their captors would think they had escaped.

It might work.

Except, as far as Von could see, there was no way to escape. Yet, hiding was the only step she could take to protect them. She couldn't do nothing.

But then how would she get up there? Being found in this room would be a surefire indication of exactly what had gone down.

Her hands settled on her waist.

She looked down.

The rope.

Inspiration had adrenaline firing in her veins.

"I need you to help me get back up there," she said to the oldest.

Renewed terror flashed in six sets of eyes.

She touched the rope at her waist. "I'm going to pull each of you up, too. But I have to get up there first."

Lips quivered and tears flowed down the cheeks of two of the girls.

Tara turned to the clutch of girls. "Listen," she whispered fiercely. "Von's here to help us. We have to listen to her. Okay?"

Little heads bobbed up and down.

Tara turned back to Von. "Tell me what to do."

It wasn't an easy task, but Von figured it out. She used the biggest of the little girls, made a pyramid/

ladder of sorts and then climbed up, trying her level best not to hurt anyone.

Once Von was on the beam, she laid down lengthwise. After snugging her legs on either side of the steel and curling one arm around it, she reached down with her right hand.

Tara, with the help of April, hefted the smallest girl up within Von's reach.

Slowly, but surely she pulled four little girls up to the beam. Her entire body was shaking with exhaustion. She'd lined the little girls up on the beam, impressing upon each one how important it was not to move. She explained how the tiles would give way if they fell against them and then they would fall to the floor.

Each sat like a little stone statue, not moving a muscle.

Von tied one end of the rope around her waist and lowered the other down to the room. It didn't quite reach the floor, but low enough that April could grab on. She climbed part of the way and Von pulled her up the rest of the way. She joined the other little ones lining the steel beam.

Tara's turn.

She was older and heavier than the others and Von was really tired but she would die before she'd leave a single child in that room.

Tara climbed as far as she could. Von pulled. The rope slipped once. But somehow Von managed to haul the child through the opening.

Before she dared to relax, Von righted the ceiling tile, careful to ensure it was exactly the way she'd found it.

It was very dark with the tile back in place. The children were terrified. But Tara did an excellent job of keeping them calm.

Von couldn't rest her muscles as long as she wanted to. She had to get moving.

"I'm going to the other room and get the rest of the children," she told Tara. "Whatever happens, don't move and don't make a sound. Do you understand me?"

Tara nodded enthusiastically.

Using the steel beam that ran across the main wall that divided the small square rooms from the large room where the captors were, Von made her way past her room and the bathroom. When she reached room number one, the first from the left, she moved onto the beam that cut across the dividing wall.

Once again, she carefully moved a ceiling tile. Again, the children huddled in fear as she attempted to lower herself into the room.

She wasn't so lucky this time. None came to her aid. There wasn't a Tara in this group.

But there was a Lily.

Relief expanded in her chest when she recognized the little girl.

She explained who she was and what she was doing to help the girls. The oldest, Jenny, finally stepped up to the plate and showed similar leadership skills as Tara had.

Climbing back up into the ceiling cavity wasn't so easy this time, either. Two of the girls were very small, including Lily. But Von finally made it.

The smallest girls were lifted up first, then the rest. Finally Jenny.

"I have to go back down now," Von explained to Jenny. "Those bad men will find me, but you must be absolutely quiet no matter what you hear happening. If they can't find you, you'll be safe."

Jenny promised to stay quiet and to keep the girls quiet.

Von shimmied back across the main beam and explained the same to Tara.

"They'll hurt you," Tara protested.

There was no time for this.

"Maybe," Von acknowledged. "But I can't help you if you don't do as I say."

Finally Tara relented and made the same promise Jenny had.

Von lowered back down onto the rickety chair. She put the ceiling tile in place, then climbed down to the floor. Moving quickly, she dismantled her climbing apparatus and put all back just as it was.

The duct tape she had used she stuck to the bottom of the cart, out of sight. The rope she placed on the cart's lowest shelf.

She brushed off her clothes. Took a breath and waited. The cameras obviously weren't operable. Not only had no one come rushing in while she went through this little rescue exercise, but she also hadn't noticed any monitors with realtime video feed in the large room.

They were in the middle of nowhere. These were children. The bastards clearly thought they had nothing to worry about.

Trinity should be back by now.

Von started to pace. She had no way of knowing what time it was, but it felt as if it had been hours.

The men's voices were louder now. Definitely arguing.

The door to her room burst open.

"You," one of the men, the older, chubby one, demanded, "get out here."

Von squared her shoulders and walked out the door, fully expecting to find Trinity and Lane back.

No Trinity.

No Lane.

Only the men who'd been here when they arrived. Judging by their expressions all were ticked off. Wait, there was one newcomer. Middle-aged. Dressed in a distinguished suit. Nothing like the others.

Was he the buyer?

"The truck is ready."

Von's gaze shifted to the female voice that had made the announcement. A young woman, twenty-two or -three at most, had entered the building and now walked quickly across the room. She glanced at

Von and then tiptoed to whisper something in Suit Guy's ear.

Blond hair...slender build...the woman looked familiar. When she turned to walk back out of the building Von studied her profile. Something about the curve of her cheek...her profile.

Von knew this woman from somewhere.

"Your husband and Lane aren't back yet," the older man with the bulging belly roared.

That was obvious. "Where are they?" she asked in a small voice. She had to remember that she was a victim here. She had to act like one. As the gazes stared holes through her, she hugged her arms around herself and tried to look frightened.

"We're going to assume that your husband caused trouble and that Lane and Robinson won't be coming back," he snapped.

Von wouldn't bank on that. "My husband would never leave me here like this. You're wrong." She tilted her chin defiantly. "I know my husband."

"Well, I don't." The older, chubby man bellied up to her. "I'm going with the theory that we've been made and we're moving now, instead of later."

This was going to get ugly.

"Let me call home," she offered in the most pitiful voice she could muster. "Or his office." She shook her head. "I'm telling you he wouldn't do this."

"No time," he snarled. "We're ready to move."

It wasn't until he made the statement that she noticed the changes in the room. There was nothing.

The desks and computers, the chairs, even the sofas. All of it was gone. Nothing but concrete floors, white walls and cheap fluorescent lights dangling from the ceilings.

"But what about the money?" Von asked. "Don't you want my husband's money?"

"Get the brats," the chubby guy ordered, ignoring her questions.

Von held her breath.

The others hurried to do as they were told.

Doors opened.

Scrambling around…surprised voices tossed questions back and forth.

Finally the announcement she'd been expecting echoed: "They're gone!"

Chubby Guy moved closer and glared at Von. "Where are they?"

She blinked, tried to look bewildered. "What're you talking about? You've had me locked in that room all this time. Where is my husband?"

"Where…are…the…children?" Each word was spat at her through clenched teeth.

"I told you I don't know what you're talking about."

"Get me those bolt cutters," he roared.

A man grabbed Von from behind.

Time to stop playing.

She whirled around and landed the heel of her hand into his throat. He stumbled back, gagging.

Another reached for her. She kicked his feet out from under him and twisted away from him.

Vicious fingers dug into her flesh, hauled her up against a hard body just as the muzzle of a weapon bored into her temple. "You've been holding out on me, missy," this one snarled.

"Tear this place apart," Chubby Guy shouted to his minions. "Find those brats. They're in here somewhere. They have to be."

It didn't take the bastards long to figure out that up was the only way to go.

Von closed her eyes at the sound of the children wailing in terror.

"I think we should let the kiddies watch you die," Chubby growled in her ear.

"Let her go."

Von's gaze shot to the man who had spoken. The guy in the pricey suit. Suit Guy.

"She and her husband have caused a lot of trouble," Chubby argued.

Suit Guy shook his head. "Nothing we can do about that now. If Lane had stuck to his agenda, this wouldn't have happened. Let her go. Now," he reiterated when his underling hesitated.

Chubby released her and Von took a challenging step toward the man in the suit. "I'm not going anywhere without those kids."

He smiled. "You may be more right than you know. Take off your coat."

Her eyes narrowed. "I don't think so." She wasn't doing anything this perv told her to do.

He nodded to his henchmen. Roughs hands peeled the coat off her shoulders and down her arms. It landed on the floor behind her.

Suit Guy walked all the way around her. The silence in the building was deafening.

He suddenly stopped and turned to Chubby. "She goes with us. She'll bring a nice sum in the gaming auction." He smiled at Von. "They love women like you. Those prepared to fight to the death."

Fury blasted any reason right out of Von's head. "I'm not going anywhere with you unless you let the children go."

"How nice," he mused aloud, "a woman willing to sacrifice herself for others. Such a rare trait."

Von lunged for the bastard.

Savage hands grabbed her back.

"You'll find out," she threatened, "just how rare I am."

A needle pierced her skin on the back of her shoulder.

Von whirled around to fight off her attacker.

She staggered as the room kept spinning.

The children were her final thought before the blackness descended.

Chapter Twelve

12:58 a.m. (11 hours missing)

Trinity's heart pounded hard enough to burst through the wall of his chest.

The house he'd spotted was a good half mile off the road.

He hadn't slowed down since he'd left Lane and his pal in the trunk of their sedan.

Not a single vehicle...not the first sign of a house until now.

Barking greeted him as he neared the house.

Two dogs, their growls several levels below friendly, circled him.

Trinity ignored the animals.

He climbed the steps, his lungs burning with the need for air, and crossed the porch. With no compunction as to the time, he banged hard enough on the door to shake the Christmas wreath hanging there and to wake the dead.

The dogs stayed close, growling and snarling.

No sound inside the house.

Trinity banged again, harder still.

A light came on inside.

Thank God.

The overhead porch light blinked on next.

With a heavy creak the door flew inward and the black muzzle of a double barrel shotgun came within inches of Trinity's face.

"What do you want?" The pajama-clad man had obviously awakened from a deep sleep. His hair was mussed and his face was grim.

That was the first time Trinity noticed exactly how cold it was. The chill leached into his bones and exhaustion clawed at him.

"I need to call for help," Trinity explained. "My wife's been abducted."

The man's gaze narrowed even more. "What do you mean abducted?"

"These men took her.... They tried to kill me." Trinity hoped that part would get this guy's full attention a little more rapidly. He needed a damned phone!

The man looked past Trinity then hitched his head in invitation. "Come on in. Ingrid!" he shouted over his shoulder. "Make some coffee."

Trinity was barely inside the door when the man gestured to the table next to the sofa. "There's the phone."

Trinity put through a call to Jim Colby and gave his location. The man with the shotgun provided specific road numbers and directions from the city.

Jim assured Trinity that he and Simon, as well as Simon's Bureau contact, were en route.

Trinity replaced the receiver and tried not to sway. Seemed the warmer he got on the outside the colder he felt on the inside.

"This'll warm you up." A woman, the wife, Ingrid, Trinity supposed, offered him a mug of steaming coffee.

"Thank you." He cradled the hot cup in his hands. As soon as he'd caught his breath he would keep going to try and find that damned barn. He couldn't wait for Simon and Jim to arrive.

Ingrid tied the sash of her robe a little more tightly. "What happened to your wife?"

Jessie, the husband, had taken a seat on the couch, but the shotgun remained propped against his leg. He sipped his coffee and eyed Trinity with slowly receding suspicion.

"We were looking for a missing child—"

"Your child is missing, too?" Ingrid asked, her voice as well as her expression loaded with disbelief.

"She's not our little girl," he explained. "She's the daughter of a friend. We were trying to help find her. The men responsible for her abduction are using what looks like a barn in the woods." He shook his head. "It can't be much farther up the road."

"You talking about the old Crosby place?" Jessie set his coffee mug on the table next to him.

Trinity shrugged. "I'm not familiar with this area.

But it looks like a barn. I didn't see a house. It's a good distance off the paved road."

"Get my coat," Jessie said to his wife. "I know the place you're talking about. I'll take you there right now. Ingrid'll tell the police or whoever you called where to go when they get here."

Trinity set his cup aside as well. "Do you have a cell phone we can take with us?"

Jessie shook his head as he shouldered into the coat Ingrid rushed to him. "But I got this shotgun and a four-wheel drive truck."

Trinity managed a smile. "That'll work."

LESS THAN TEN MINUTES on the dark road and Jessie turned on his left blinker. "This is the old Crosby place."

"This is it." Trinity recognized the big oak tree that loomed close to the narrow dirt road that cut into the woods. The oak was long dead. It was a miracle it hadn't already fallen.

"Couple months ago I was down this way and saw a truck waiting to pull out on the road," Jessie said. "I figured the place had been sold. Never bothered to come over here and see what was going on or ask nobody."

"Let's take it a little slow," Trinity suggested.

Jessie cut the headlights. "No use warning 'em that we're coming."

The narrow road gave way to a clearing and what looked like an old barn stood beneath the moonlight, surrounded by snow—snow that had been heavily marred by tire tracks.

The SUVs he'd noticed here before were gone.

"Stop," Trinity said, desperation aching in his chest.

He hoped out of the truck and bounded through the snow. The big double doors opened with no resistance. The barn was dark but Trinity could feel the emptiness.

They were gone.

He motioned for Jessie to pull closer then shouted, "Turn on your headlights."

The twin beams of light split through the dark interior of the building. The desks, chairs…everything was gone.

Trinity found the wall switch and turned on the fluorescent lights. The harsh glare reflected against the white walls and bare cement floor.

He moved from door to door at the far end of the building. Each was empty, but oddly in shambles. The ceiling tiles were pulled down here and there. He had a feeling that Von had something to do with that.

The place was completely deserted.

He turned back to Jessie. "Did you say your truck is four-wheel drive?"

"Yes, sir."

"I need you to drive me around the building…" Trinity exhaled a breath of sheer misery. "So I can see if there's anything out there."

"Got spotlights, too," Jessie explained as they hustled back to his truck.

He drove slowly around the clearing, shining his spotlights and headlights so that Trinity could search for anything...or anyone left behind.

Nothing.

Simon and Jim would likely be here any minute. Trinity couldn't wait.

"Can you take me one more place?" he asked Jessie.

"THAT IT?" JESSIE ASKED.

"That's it."

Lane's car.

"Pull over here and leave your emergency flashers on." Since he didn't have a cell phone he needed to catch Jim and Simon's attention when they passed. Since they hadn't met a single vehicle on the road, Trinity could safely assume they were still en route.

Trinity bounded out of the truck and snagged the keys from the car's ignition.

Jessie shut down the truck's engine but left the lights on as well as the flashers. Trinity could hear the men kicking at the trunk and swearing at each other.

"Friends of yours?" Jessie asked.

Trinity shook his head. "They know who took my wife." He kept calling Von his wife even though that cover was no longer necessary...but the truth was he'd always thought of her as his wife.

"They armed?"

He shook his head again and opened his jacket. "I have their weapons."

Jessie pulled the shotgun away from his shoulder where he had it propped and aimed the barrel at the trunk. "Open'er up and let's see what they got to say."

"My thoughts exactly." Trinity drew the weapon with the most ammo in the clip with his right hand and unlocked the trunk with his left.

Both men attempted to sit up.

"Don't move," Trinity warned.

"You're a dead man," Lane challenged.

"You might want to reassess that conclusion," Jessie suggested.

Trinity liked this guy better all the time.

"Get out," Trinity ordered.

When both men attempted to do so, Trinity aimed the weapon at Lane. "Not you."

The other guy scrambled out over his boss.

Trinity slammed the trunk lid closed and turned to the man whose teeth were chattering from the cold. "What's your name?"

"Waylon Robinson."

"Okay, Robinson," Trinity said, "on your knees."

"Look, man," the guy whined, "I'll tell you whatever you want to know. Just don't do this."

"You heard him," Jessie echoed. "On the ground."

The guy lowered to his knees, fear seeping from his pores like sweat.

"Where did they take my wife?"

The idiot's eyes went even wider. "They left?"

"Yes." Trinity rammed the muzzle into his forehead. "Where did they go? They must've had a plan. A route. A rendezvous with a buyer. Tell me now. This is the only chance you'll get."

"Okay, okay. I don't know about your wife, but they have to get the kids to New Orleans by Christmas morning. The buyer takes them by boat from there. I don't know where to. I swear to God." He closed his eyes and shook his head. "That's all I know. I just do what I'm told."

Trinity felt sick to his stomach that these bastards would be doing this disgusting work at all, but especially at Christmas. "I need to know what they're traveling in and the route."

The guy's eyes opened wide. "Sometimes it's a panel truck. Sometimes a van. It was always different, just like the route."

Lane's ranting inside the trunk grew increasingly louder.

Had to be a good eighteen hours from here to New Orleans. "They make any regular stops?"

"Just one." His face turned somber.

"Where?"

"I'll show you, but I'm not telling you."

Well, damn. The scumbag had grown a brain in the last five minutes. Great.

"I'd just go ahead and shoot him," Jessie suggested, the aim of his double barrel centered on the man's head. "He don't seem worth saving to me."

"You're probably right," Trinity agreed. "But I would like to get my wife back before Christmas."

"I can take you straight there. If we hurry, we'll beat them there and we can take 'em by surprise. There'll only be two in the truck. We got time to get there first before anyone shows."

"Since they've left already," Trinity wondered, "why didn't they stop and pick up you and Lane? They surely would've recognized your vehicle. It's not like there's much traffic on this stretch of road."

He shook his head adamantly. "They never leave in this direction." He hitched his head south. "They take the back roads to the interstate."

"What's the purpose of this one stop they make?" Trinity still wasn't convinced.

"To pick up more merchandise. They got two streams of supply. One here and one down south. They'll meet up with their counterparts down there and then you'll be seriously outnumbered."

Headlights coming from the north cut through the darkness.

"Think maybe that's your friends?" Jessie asked.

"Hope so." Trinity turned to watch the car approach.

As it slowed to a stop he recognized Simon Ruhl behind the wheel. Relief made his knees weak.

WHEN SIMON, JIM, AND FBI AGENT George White were brought up to speed, Trinity suggested a strategy.

"Robinson will take me to the next pick up location—the only other stop between here and New Orleans—and I'll intercept with the help of local law enforcement, if necessary."

White was shaking his head before Trinity finished his statement. "I can't let you do this without the Bureau. This is a federal crime, Colby," he said to Jim. "The Bureau has jurisdiction."

Trinity wasn't wasting time arguing. "Then you'll go with us."

"Wait!" Robinson argued. "I said I'd take you. I'm not taking no fed."

"First of all—" White countered Trinity, ignoring Robinson all together "—we should have notified the local authorities already. The lives of twelve minors are at stake. We're all in violation of at least a half dozen laws."

Jim held up his hands before anyone else could speak. "Agent White is absolutely right." When Trinity would have balked, Jim went on, "However, we need a head start if we're going to ensure the safety of these children as well as Von."

"What do you have in mind?" White asked, clearly still unconvinced.

"Simon," Jim turned to the man at his side, "call Ian and have him bring an SUV with everything Barrett will need. We need it here ASAP. And call your contact at the paper and see if we can slip in a last-minute bit of breaking news in the morning edition. We want whoever is behind this to believe Lane and Robinson didn't survive to be interrogated by authorities."

Simon pulled his cell phone from his jacket and stepped aside to make the calls.

Lane started to grunt and groan around the glove that had been stuffed into his mouth. He'd been taken from the trunk and set on the ground until a decision was made.

"What're you up to, Colby?" White demanded.

"You and Barrett will get on the road with your guide here and intercept these bastards. So that they won't change their strategy, we'll make sure the news mentions that a car with two unidentified dead bodies was discovered in the wee hours of the morning."

White nodded. "I see where you're going."

"All we need is thirty-six hours," Trinity said. "Once we've intercepted the cargo, White can have the New Orleans field office set a trap for the buyer at the port. There won't be any collateral damage and the Bureau gets a big break in this operation."

White held up his hands. "All right." He exhaled a heavy breath. "That I'll agree to. But only because I can write it up as part of my ongoing investigation."

"What about him?" Trinity nodded toward Lane.

"I'm certain my friends at Chicago PD can figure out something to do with him for the next thirty-six hours," Jim offered. "And you," he said to Robinson, "may get full immunity for your cooperation."

Lane started that emphatic grunting and groaning again. Jim nodded to Trinity who removed the man's gag.

"I'll cooperate," he said. "I waive my right to counsel just like Robinson. I want to help."

"Considering the delicacy and shortness of time," White said, "I will allow you to remain in Mr. Colby and Mr. Ruhl's custody for the next thirty-six hours. During which time you will be represented by counsel and will give a full accounting of all you know related to this operation. That's how you can help, Lane."

"Anything," Lane pleaded.

"Be aware," White reminded both men, "that I do not have the authority to grant either of you immunity, but I can vouch for your cooperation and if we're successful in returning these children unharmed, I believe your efforts will be recognized."

"Close enough," Lane agreed.

Simon stepped back into the circle. "Ian is making the necessary preparations and I've made the calls to ensure the media works to our advantage."

Trinity wasn't sure he could stand waiting another minute.

Jim turned to him. "You find Von and bring her and those children back here unharmed."

Trinity nodded. "Yes, sir."

He would do it or die trying.

Chapter Thirteen

The roar of the wheels on the asphalt had finally lulled the children to sleep.

The tranquillizer they'd used on Von had worn off an hour or so ago. Since then she'd dozed once or twice but she'd jerked awake each time the momentum of the vehicle changed.

The bastards had provided blankets and pillows. Otherwise they lay on the cold steel bed of the panel truck. A case of bottled water and a small portable toilet had been provided.

More frightening, they were smashed into a small area near the cab while office furniture filled the end nearest the side-by-side cargo doors. The furniture appeared to be attached to the walls of the cargo area, but if any of it came loose and the driver made a sudden stop the children could be... She didn't even want to think about it.

The risks these people took with the lives of these children were appalling. What was she thinking? They had no sense of compassion for these children. These little girls were commodities.

She and the children had been warned that if they tried anything or made any noise, especially when the vehicle was stopped, they would all die. Von looked around the walls and ceiling of the cargo area in an attempt to see through the semi-darkness. The driver had warned that explosives were rigged in the cargo area. If she and the children failed to behave…they would be remotely activated.

Von hoped she lived long enough to personally beat the attitude out of at least one of these scumbags. Preferably the guy in the suit.

Trinity.

She wouldn't believe he was dead.

He was far too resourceful for that.

Knowing him, he was hot on the trail of this damned truck right now.

Except he didn't know what kind of vehicle they were in or what route they had taken. Or their destination, for that matter.

No one beyond the people involved in this heinous act did.

Maybe Lane or his cohort knew, but expecting either one of them to talk, assuming they were still alive, was likely wishful thinking.

If they were dead…Trinity might be alive.

An ache swelled in her chest.

She didn't love him anymore. The very idea, after five years, would be ridiculous. But she didn't want anything bad to happen to him.

But they were over. Way over.

After five years she had come to the conclusion that what happened was not his fault any more than it was hers. They had been young...it had just happened.

She'd lost the baby. Three months pregnant and... she'd lost it. He hadn't forced her to go to work that day. It had been her decision. That he'd gotten caught in traffic and hadn't made the rendezvous in time hadn't been his fault. She had known it then but it had been a lot easier to blame him than to blame herself. And in all likelihood it was just random bad luck.

Her entire life, everything she'd loved had been taken from her. Her father in a freak car accident when she was five and then her mother from cancer when Von had only been thirteen. On Christmas Eve, at that.

Where had God been when she'd needed him?

Time had passed and she'd let it go. It hadn't been God's fault. It just was. Von had made up her mind that it was best not to let herself care too much about anything. No risk involved that way.

Then she'd met Trinity. She'd fallen so hard for him. She'd been eighteen and full of eagerness to explore every aspect of life.

Two weeks later they had gotten married. So, painfully young. So very much in love.

They'd worked for a friend of Trinity's in the bail bonding business. Von had loved her work...loved even more that she worked most of the time with Trinity.

She shouldn't haven taken the same old risks after discovering she was pregnant. She should have been more careful.

Her hand went to her abdomen as if, even now, she could feel the pain. God had let her down again. She hadn't trusted Him since.

Just stop.

Von cleared the past from her mind and summoned the image of the blonde from back at the transfer facility. Von knew that face. But for the life of her she couldn't think from where.

A whimper drew her attention to Lily. The lighting was dim, but Von's eyes had adjusted hours ago.

The whimpers evolved into sobs and Von crawled over to where she lay. If the other girls woke, she'd have a real problem on her hands.

"Hey." She swept a wisp of blond hair from the little girl's damp cheek. "You can't sleep?" Von knew that considering all the child had been through with her insane father and then these criminals it was no wonder she was having nightmares.

Lily shook her head. "I'm scared the bombs'll go off."

Bastards. "We're okay right now. Here." Von scooted in next to her and pulled the child against her chest. "Maybe we can go to sleep together."

"I want my mommy," Lily murmured.

Von swiped the tears from Lily's cheek. "Well, I just happen to know that your mommy's looking forward to seeing you, too. She'll be waiting for you when we get back home."

"What about the bad men?" Lily whispered. "They said we can't go back home."

"You don't worry about what those bad men say," Von said firmly. "I'm taking all of you home. Now, let's go to sleep."

"Tell me a story?"

Von wanted to say no. She'd put children's stories and all that stuff out of her mind a long time ago.

"Please, Miss Von," another little voice said. "Tell us a story."

"My stories aren't very good," Von hedged. How the heck had she gotten into a situation like this? She didn't even like kids. Not really. She'd made the decision after losing her baby. It made life simpler. Besides, she was a career-focused single woman.

And she liked it that way.

Pleas echoed around the group that was supposed to be sleeping.

She was outnumbered.

"Fine, fine," Von surrendered. "I'll tell you a story, but then someone has to tell me a story."

One that involved Trinity showing up to save the day.

Now where had that thought come from?

"Once upon a time," she began.

"Not that kind of story," Tara protested.

Now they were going to tell her how to *tell* the story?

"When I was a kid," Von cautioned the girls, "all good stories started with once upon a time."

"We want to hear your story," April said.

"Did the bad men ever take you when you were a little girl?" another asked.

She could tell them the one her aunt had told her, that God had taken Von's mother on Christmas Eve because he needed another angel. Or the one about how Von couldn't stay with her aunt and cousins because they didn't have enough room. Foster homes were far better for little orphaned girls.

Or maybe she should tell the one about how she'd lost the one thing she'd wanted more than anything else in this whole wide world—her baby.

How life wasn't fair.

How no one could be trusted with your heart.

"Miss Von?"

Von blinked away the bad memories. "Okay. How about I tell you about my adventures as Von the superhero?"

"You're a superhero?" Tara asked.

"Like in the movies?" Lily wanted to know.

"Maybe not that super," Von confessed, "but I've had my share of adventures where I rescued someone in trouble." She'd failed as a daughter and a wife and a mother. But she was damned good as a rescuer.

"Like when you tried to hide us from the bad men?" April asked.

"Yeah," Von said. "And like I'm here with you

right now. I'm not leaving you. I'll keep trying to rescue you until I get the job done."

And she would.

No matter how badly her childhood, or any other aspect of her life, had stunk. Von Cassidy was a good guy—gal. She rescued those who needed rescuing.

That was her job.

If she were really, really lucky, Trinity would show up to give her a hand.

"There was a little girl named Evonne," she began. "She couldn't spell her name so her mom shortened it to Von."

Giggles rippled around the group.

"When she was only six years old and in first grade she had to rescue a white rabbit."

A dozen questions bombarded her. What was the rabbit's name? Where did she go to kindergarten? How big was the rabbit? Did the rabbit have a mom and dad? And so on.

As Von lost herself to the silly story of the last week of first grade, she couldn't help thinking that her poor old teacher had about lost her mind trying to find that darned rabbit.

Maybe some parts of her childhood weren't so bad.

If she lived through this she would have to tell Trinity the rabbit story.

Chapter Fourteen

"Jim."

Jim roused from a deep sleep, the first he'd had in twenty-four hours. He straightened and blinked. He'd fallen asleep at his desk. "What's wrong? Have we heard from Barrett or Von?"

"Nothing yet." Ian Michaels stood at his door. "But we may have a situation."

Jim had known Ian Michaels for a long time. He and Simon Ruhl were seconds in command here at the agency. A former U.S. Marshal, Ian was as dark and mysterious as was Simon, former FBI, but both men were the best in the business of private investigations. If Ian thought they had a situation, then they had a serious situation.

"We need you in the conference room."

Jim jumped from his chair and strode across the room. When he'd come to his office for some shut-eye, Simon Ruhl had still been interrogating Lane.

Apparently he'd learned something new. "What's going on?"

"Lane claims he has some additional information that he'd forgotten until now."

Jim shook his head. "Yeah, right. Has Simon had any sleep?"

"Very little. He's had misgivings about Lane's statement from the beginning. At this point, he's quite frustrated."

Jim was aware that Simon wasn't convinced of the man's story. He'd left Simon with the job of digging the truth out of him. "I guess we'll find out what Lane's been hiding."

In the conference room, Simon sat at the long table with Lane. "He refused to talk," Simon explained, "until you were in the room." The frustration Ian had spoken of vibrated in his tone.

Jim pulled out a chair and sat down. Ian did the same. "All right, Lane. You have our attention. What is it you have to add that's so important?"

"I've been thinking about the activities of the past few months." Lane pursed his lips and appeared to give his next words deep thought before continuing. "There have been times during the past few operations that I felt the orders I received were influenced by someone who has an in with law enforcement."

An alarm triggered deep inside Jim. "You have three seconds to get to the point, Lane, or this will not end well. You have my word on that."

Ian and Simon exchanged a look of concern but neither objected.

They should be worried. Jim would not play games with this lowlife. He could either come clean now or Jim would be cleaning the floor with his face.

"I believe my superior was notified when and how certain attempts to bring down our operation would be carried out. It seemed to me that we always brushed right past any such attempts."

"Someone in Chicago PD?" Jim prompted.

Lane stared straight into Jim's eyes. "I want full immunity. I know your agency. You have the power and influence to make that happen."

Jim shifted his attention to Simon and Ian. "Would you gentlemen excuse us for a moment?"

"Jim," Ian said, "we should—"

"Now," Jim interrupted. He wanted no witnesses to what he was about to do and say. He definitely didn't want to involve Ian or Simon in his decision to cross the line. And he was definitely about to cross the line.

With obvious reluctance, the two men stood and left the room, closing the door behind them.

Jim pushed up from his chair and walked around to Lane's side of the table.

To say the man's cocky attitude had melted into one of nervous uncertainty would be an understatement.

In one swift, fluid motion, Jim shoved Lane's head against the polished mahogany table. He withdrew the weapon from his waistband and rammed it into the man's skull. "If you know something that affects the well-being of my two investigators you'd better tell me now."

"It's the fed," Lane croaked hoarsely. "Agent White. He's the inside guy. I guarantee the only reason he went along with this whole thing was so he could ensure your people failed. He's the one who told me this Barton couple's intention to buy a kid was a setup. If he doesn't kill them, he'll make sure someone else does."

Jim leaned down close and whispered in Lane's ear. "You'd better pray that you haven't waited too long to come clean. I'd hate for housecleaning to have to scrape your brains off my mother's shiny conference table."

Jim shoved the weapon back into his waistband and reached for the phone.

Maybe it wasn't too late to warn Trinity.

Chapter Fifteen

I-65 South, 10:05 a.m.

Twenty miles to Huntsville, Alabama.

Trinity had broken the speed limit by fifteen to twenty miles per hour for most of the trip.

Robinson was asleep in the passenger seat. White sat in the backseat and, like Trinity, had refused to take his eyes off the road or his attention off the operation.

His cell phone had died hours ago. He'd been using Trinity's most of the morning since he had charging capabilities. Giving the guy grace, White hadn't had someone like Ian Michaels making trip preparations for him. Ian had pretty much thought of everything.

Trinity gave Robinson a shake. "Wake up, man. I think the next exit is ours."

Robinson sat up straighter and rubbed a hand over his face. "Yeah, that's it." He pointed to the upcoming exit. Then he peered at the time on the dash. "We should be running just ahead of the truck. They can't risk speeding, for obvious reasons."

Trinity slowed for the exit, merged onto the 565 interchange and accelerated. He couldn't get there fast enough. Determination to get Von back from those bastards and to rescue the children was all that had kept him going the past eight hours when sleep and exhaustion had relentlessly haunted him.

Finding her safe and getting her back to Chicago, along with the children, was his top priority. He would not fail her or those kids.

"The pickup location is a condemned mill," Robinson said. "It's in an old, rundown part of town. Don't have to worry about anybody getting in your business around there."

"We just stay out of sight until the truck or van arrives?" Trinity couldn't get right with the idea that those in charge were going to move forward with their game plan despite last night's glitch.

The organization was tightly run. They hadn't been caught yet and there was a reason for that.

They didn't make stupid mistakes.

Something was off kilter.

"Yeah. When they arrive, there will be a delay before moving out again," Robinson explained. "They'll wait until after midnight."

"Why wait that late?" That didn't add up considering their current movements, if the cover of darkness was the point. "They've been on the road all morning."

"We usually get on the road earlier so we're on location by dawn. Last night was off because Lane wanted to make some extra cash. He gave the boss an excuse about not being prepared." Robinson stretched his back as best he could within the confines of the vehicle. "We don't usually take this kind of risk. The middle of the night is way better. Traffic's light and cops are usually sleeping in their cars."

White received another call. Trinity glanced in the rearview mirror. The agent appeared in deep conversation.

Whether it was sleep deprivation or paranoia motivated by exhaustion and worry, this just didn't feel right to Trinity. That feeling was escalating with every passing hour. Getting on the road after the bastards who had Von and the kids had been his sole goal after midnight last night. But now, maybe because the adrenaline had slowed, his instincts were screaming at him.

"That was Simon," White said. "Lane has given a very detailed statement. His story confirms what Robinson has told us thus far."

Trinity felt some amount of relief at hearing from Simon. "Did you bring him up to speed on our progress?"

"I did. We're to give him a heads-up when we get into position."

Robinson leaned forward. "We got a few more minutes before we get to the next exit. I need a restroom and some coffee."

"That wouldn't be a bad idea," White agreed. "Get that part over before we reach our destination."

Trinity didn't want to stop, didn't want to take the time. So far they'd only gotten off the road for fuel, taking relief breaks at the same time. But time was on their side at this point. A rest stop couldn't hurt. He needed to be ready to act once they were in position at the target location.

"Take the next exit," Robinson said as he pulled the gloves from his coat pockets and tucked them into place. "It's a truck stop. Always plenty of traffic. Makes it easy to remain anonymous." He picked up the scarf hanging loosely on his shoulders and wrapped it around his throat as if he expected icy winds.

Frustration creeping under his skin, Trinity took the exit. It was a good twenty degrees warmer here, he didn't see any reason for gloves or a scarf. But then, he was obsessing on insignificant details.

"That one," Robinson said, "on the right."

The truck stop was massive. Thirteen or fourteen pump islands surrounded a large building. Like Robinson said it was plenty crowded. "You been here before," Trinity ventured.

"Lots of times."

When Trinity's booted feet hit the ground, he took a moment to stretch. Almost nine hours behind the wheel had stiffened his muscles.

Not about to let Robinson out of his sight, Trinity followed the guy and White through the building's main entrance. Just inside the double doors there were two more sets of double doors, one to the convenience store on the left and the other to a restaurant on the right, a narrow corridor leading to the restrooms cut straight through the middle.

"I gotta hit the john first," Robinson said, heading into the corridor.

White nodded, going in the same direction.

Though a large cup of coffee would be damned good right now, Trinity hesitated a moment—he preferred to stick with Robinson. He couldn't afford to risk losing him. Right now, the sleaze was Trinity's only connection to getting Von back. And the children.

Inside the men's room was the usual equipment with numerous stalls and a couple of showers. For the truckers, he supposed. White was taking care of business at one of the urinals already.

Trinity checked the bottom of the stalls until he saw Robinson's shoes, then chose the urinal closest to the exit so he'd be between Robinson and the exit when he emerged from his stall.

White strolled over to the row of sinks and Robinson stepped out of the stall. The fact that he didn't flush caused Trinity to hesitate before taking care of his own needs.

Robinson pulled his scarf higher on his face as he walked up behind White.

"Robinson, what—?"

He grabbed the agent around the neck.

Trinity lunged in that direction.

Robinson snatched White's weapon from his shoulder holster and fired a round into the agent's temple. The muffled ping echoed in the room.

Trinity reached for the weapon in his waistband.

Robinson released the agent's body and thrust the muzzle of the weapon in Trinity's face. "Think before you act, Barrett."

Trinity glared at him. "What the hell have you done?" Ignoring his own safety, he lowered to a crouch and checked White's carotid artery. Damn. Half the man's skull was missing.

Robinson kicked White's shoulder. "Don't waste your time. He's dead."

Fury and shock making his movements stilted, Trinity searched White's pockets for his cell phone.

Where the hell was it?

The sound of paper towels being torn from the roll jerked Trinity's attention upward. He leveled a bead on Robinson. "Put the gun down, you son of a bitch."

Robinson wiped the blood splatters from his hands and tossed the soiled paper towel as well as the weapon to the floor. More blood and tissue clung to the wall and mirror above the sink.

"We don't have time to play this game." Gone was the frightened hired helper who just wanted immunity or a lighter sentence. The man staring at Trinity had the look and sound of a ruthless killer. He unwound the scarf from his neck and poked it into the trash bin.

"You killed a federal agent," Trinity roared. He snatched up the weapon Robinson had tossed. "You're not going anywhere but into official custody."

Robinson laughed. "You won't do that."

"Watch me." Trinity pushed to his feet. All he had to do was walk into the convenience store or the restaurant and have someone—anyone—call the police. Robinson was out of his mind if he thought Trinity was going to let him get away with this. He wouldn't kill him because he needed him.

"You can't save your friend and all those children if you kill me or have me locked up."

Robinson started for the door, turning his back to Trinity and the weapon leveled on him. The man definitely had to be insane. "Stop," Trinity ordered.

A hand on the door, Robinson turned back to him. "You see that?" He nodded to the weapon he'd used to kill White. "Why do you suppose Agent White put a silencer on his weapon? You don't have one on yours."

Trinity hadn't missed the silencer. He hadn't seen White attach the silencer. Hadn't heard him mention needing one. It certainly wasn't standard issue.

"He's one of them," Robinson said. "He was going to kill you when we got to the location. Me, too, probably. Now, let's go."

"I can't leave him here." Trinity shook his head. "I

have to call the police. You will give me the location and then I'm calling the police."

Robinson shrugged. "Go ahead. Then you'll be detained and questioned. God only knows how long that will take. Not to mention—" he nodded to the weapon once more "—it has your prints on it, not mine." He held up a gloved hand. "Meanwhile your lady friend and those children will disappear." He smiled, the expression patronizing. "I know these people, Barrett. You won't ever find her. That's assuming you aren't rotting away in prison for murdering a federal agent."

"Why should I trust you?" Trinity didn't have to mention that there was a dead man lying on the dingy tile floor that seemed to indicate otherwise. The voice of justice and morality was screaming in his brain… but Von…and those children…needed him.

"Because I don't care about you," Robinson said, "or the people you're trying to stop. I know where Lane hid the 80k you gave him. He has his own special savings account. Since he won't need it, I plan to use it for a very long, very tropical vacation."

Trinity glanced down at White once more. How could he be sure Robinson was right about him? And even if he was, this was wrong…to walk away and leave him here was unconscionable.

"He would've left you here on the floor," Robinson said, as if reading Trinity's mind. "If not here, at our next stop. The bad guys would get away. You and I would be dead and White would have been wounded.

Not to mention whatever tidy sums he received under the table for his cooperation. On top of all that, he'd be a hero for trying to stop this thing from going down. They give agents merit badges for that sort of thing, don't they?"

"Let's go." Trinity swallowed back the bitter bile of self-disgust as he put first one then the other weapon in his waistband beneath his coat.

His heart pounded so hard the blood roared in his ears as they exited that long narrow corridor. The sun seemed to spotlight Trinity as he approached the SUV. He kept expecting someone to scream and fingers to point.

They reached the SUV and Robinson held out his hand. The gloves were gone. Trinity hadn't noticed him taking them off.

"Give me the keys. I'll take it from here," Robinson said. "I know the way and you don't look your best just now."

Trinity handed him the keys and climbed into the passenger seat.

What difference did it make?

He'd crossed a line that no man on the side of right should ever cross.

Robinson pulled out onto the road and took the ramp back to the interchange. "We'll be there in less than twenty minutes. You should have plenty of time to get into position before they arrive."

Trinity shook himself. He had to contact Simon. "I

need my cell." He unfastened his seatbelt and twisted around to dig around in the backseat.

"I doubt you'll find it." Robinson snickered. "White isn't that dumb."

White's phone lay on the seat. The battery was fully charged. Fury tightened Trinity's lips. He tapped a few keys. "Damn it." Had to have a pass code.

Trinity collapsed into his seat. Robinson was probably right. Trinity's phone would be missing. White had likely disposed of it in the men's room back there before Trinity came in. He should have thought of that.

But why?

He'd had no reason to believe White was a traitor.

"What proof do you have that White was the inside man for this organization?" Trinity's voice echoed hollowly in the vehicle.

"I've seen him in secret meetings with Lane. He's the way we avoided law enforcement." Robinson slowed for an exit. "But you don't have to take my word for it. Lane has kept a file on White. He thought he might need it sometime. He can give you all the proof you need. Besides, how do you think we knew you and your wife weren't real buyers?"

Trinity couldn't help staring at the man. He wanted to rip him apart with his bare hands. "How do you sleep at night? These are children? All you care about is the money?"

"Look." Robinson shot him a glare. "I'm doing the

right thing this time. Yeah, I'm taking the money and I'm going far away. But you don't get it." He braked for the intersection at the bottom of the ramp. "This isn't the kind of job you give notice and walk away from. I've been involved in this group for three years and the only people I've seen leave have been with a bullet in the back of their skulls."

Trinity had no sympathy for him.

"Three years?" he asked. "You've watched a lot of kids snatched from their families."

Robinson had nothing to say to that.

Trinity stared out at the rundown and abandoned houses flanking the narrow street Robinson had turned onto.

Tomorrow was Christmas Eve.

Agent White was dead, whether he deserved it or not. His family would be devastated.

Twelve children from the Chicago area were missing, their parents frantic.

And Von… She might not even be alive.

She couldn't die like this. God wouldn't do that twice.

Chapter Sixteen

The truck stopped.

Von snapped to attention. She'd been dozing. The girls had all fallen asleep again and Von had surrendered to the need herself.

She'd told stories for hours. She'd even talked each of the girls into telling a story of her own.

A door slammed.

Von's breath caught.

It had been hours since they had stopped for fuel. She'd smelled petroleum fumes so she had suspected the two stops had been for fuel.

But she didn't smell anything now.

She wanted to move but two of the girls' heads were resting in her lap.

Another door slammed.

With the engine of the truck shutoff, the cargo area was dark. Really dark.

If the girls awoke now, they would be terrified.

Von licked her lips. She needed more water but she'd resisted the urge to drink her fill so the kids would have all they wanted. Still, it wasn't enough. Two bottles for each child. Very little was left.

The silence tugged at her attention.

Where were they?

They'd been on the road for a long time. Eight or more hours, she felt certain.

Had they reached their destination?

Von could sit here in fear...or she could do something.

Do something had always been her preferred choice.

If there actually were explosives rigged in this space, then she was dooming the children to sudden death. If she sat here and did nothing she was sentencing them to a fate perhaps far worse.

One at a time, Von eased the sleeping children away from her lap. She couldn't see anything. What she had been able to see when the dim lighting had been on was basically nothing. The lighting had been focused on the floor area, leaving the overhead area in total darkness.

Feeling her way, she crept to the wall of furniture that separated their compartment from the door. She pushed at it. It didn't budge.

Tracing with her fingers, she found narrow gaps and ledges. This was actual furniture put together to conceal what was behind it. She tiptoed, reached as high as possible and found a little ledge. Then she climbed, putting the toe of her shoe into a lower gap and using her fingers to pull upward from the higher ledge.

The stack of furniture didn't go all the way to the top of the cargo area. There was maybe fourteen or so inches of space.

She hauled herself up on top of the stack. Grabbed on with both arms when she almost rolled off the other side. If she made herself very straight, keeping her arms tight against her sides, she could lay there and maybe not be seen by anyone opening the cargo doors.

Something heavy moved.

A metal on metal grind pierced the air.

Von stilled. She urged her breathing and her heart to be quiet.

The side-by-side cargo doors swung outward.

The girls started to whimper and cry out for her.

Von's chest ached.

Did she go to the girls or be still?

The beam of two flashlights shone into the truck.

Von held her breath.

"Get the woman," one of the guys said. "Let's have some fun."

More creaking and scraping accompanied the moving of the portion of the stacked furniture that served as a door. Thankfully the part she wasn't lying on. These guys had gone to a lot of trouble to make it look like they were hauling a load of office furniture.

One of the men moved into the space with the girls.

Von could scarcely bear their cries.

"She's not here!" the guy stumbling around the girls shouted.

"Are you blind?" the other guy demanded as he climbed into the truck. "She has to be in there!"

Both were in the compartment with the girls.

The girls wailed. The men swore and stumbled around.

Von lowered herself down the front side of the wall of furniture and scrambled out of the truck.

It was dark.

Light tried to creep in through cracks in high walls.

No time to figure it out.

She ducked under the truck, hid behind the rear wheels on the driver's side.

The ground was dusty...not ground, she realized. Concrete.

They were in some sort of huge building.

It smelled old and burned...like charred wood.

The sobbing and wailing in the truck ripped her heart to shreds. Von put her hands over her ears to try and block the sound. She bit down on her lip, hard, to distract her brain from the horrifying sounds.

More ranting from the men.

When they came out of the truck looking for her... it wouldn't take them long to find her.

She felt over her head. Metal...caked dirt. She

crept toward the center of the vehicle. A long, round pole-like object ran down the center. Why hadn't she studied auto mechanics in high school instead of stupid home economics?

Holding her breath once more, she grabbed something that felt like metal and pulled her body lengthwise onto the long thing that extended along a good portion of the center of the vehicle.

Boots hit the concrete.

Von concentrated hard on holding on to whatever was overhead with her hands and maintaining balance on the pole.

Flashlight beams roamed, bouncing on the floor.

If she could just stay still…just be absolutely quiet…

"Idiot, you left the side door open!" one of the men growled.

What door? Von hadn't seen any door.

"I didn't leave the door open," the other argued. The statement was followed by a string of profanities from the accuser.

"Look around outside. If she gets away we're dead meat."

One of the men remained close. She heard his every step. He didn't seem concerned with stealth.

Light roved the floor beneath her.

The air evaporated in her lungs.

Don't move. Don't breathe.

The yellow beam moved away.

Von dared to breathe.

More cursing echoed in the darkness.

The truck shifted.

He was climbing back into the cargo area.

The children began to shriek and cry again.

Von closed her eyes and fought the emotions tearing at her. She had to stay still…had to make them believe she had gotten away.

Something slammed in the truck.

Remaining still was one of the hardest things Von had ever done.

Boots hit the ground again, then stormed away from the truck.

"She's not in here," one of the men shouted.

Von could hear them arguing outside.

Did she dare move?

Not yet.

A minute more…see what happened next.

Then she knew what to do…or what to try to do.

She counted backward from one hundred…then she dropped her feet to the floor and rolled off the pole. Listening for the return of the men, she scrambled from beneath the truck and headed for the cab. The door opened with no resistance. Thankfully the dome light didn't glow to life.

Her fingers went immediately to the ignition…not on the steering column. Her heart rocketed into her throat. She felt around on the dash…found it.

The key was in the ignition on the dash.

Von climbed into the seat, eased the door shut and

locked it. She scrambled across the seat and locked the passenger door as well.

Once she started the engine there would be no turning back. She had to assume that, based on the way the truck was parked, they had pulled into the building. Which meant the doorway was behind her.

As old and decrepit as this building smelled, surely the door wouldn't be that difficult to break down.

She checked the emergency brake. It was released. Stretching her legs, she checked the pedals. Brake pedal. Accelerator. Relief jangled through her. She didn't want to deal with a clutch.

"This is it," she mumbled.

As soon as they heard the engine they would run back inside, guns blazing.

Von pumped the accelerator for good measure.

She twisted the key in the ignition.

The engine growled to life.

With a yank she pulled the gearshift into Reverse, then slammed her right foot down on the accelerator.

The truck jerked backward.

Shouting.

She couldn't understand the words but she heard shouting.

The truck hit something...bounced a little. She pressed harder on the accelerator. The tires spun.

"Go, damn you!" she muttered.

The windshield shattered.

She jerked.

Her fingers scrambled across the dash for the light switch. She pulled. The lights blared on, blinding the men with the guns.

The doors hadn't given way.

To hell with it.

She let off the gas and simultaneously jerked the gearshift into Drive.

Von stomped the accelerator.

The truck jolted forward.

The men scattered.

Wall.

Damn.

She hit the brake, slammed back into Reverse, rammed the accelerator.

The truck whined but roared backward.

She hit what she hoped were the doors.

Metal groaned. Wood splintered.

The vehicle broke through the barrier and barreled backward into the open.

Sunlight blinded her for a moment.

Squinting, she tried to inventory her surroundings.

She slammed on the brakes.

Parking lot.

She was in a parking lot outside a massive run-down building.

Where were the two goons?

Too quiet.

Von shifted into Drive.

Movement.

Someone in the building.

She hit the gas and bolted across the parking lot. The turn onto the street that ran parallel to the lot almost tipped the truck over. Von didn't slow down. She had to get away.

Save the children.

What time was it? Where the hell was she? Could they really blow the truck up? They'd claimed to have explosives planted in the cargo area.

She kept driving.

More closed and dilapidated businesses flanked the narrow street.

No people.

No houses.

In the distance she could see taller buildings, not quite skyscrapers but taller than these rundown businesses. How did she get there?

She worked up the nerve to glance at her side mirrors. The street behind her was clear.

Her immediate need was a phone.

Call the police. Call the agency.

Check on Trinity.

Her heart knocked against her sternum.

The kids were probably scared to death but she didn't dare stop to explain what was happening.

Not until she was either on official police property or surrounded by police cruisers.

A big orange-and-white-striped guardrail crossed the street a block ahead.

The street ended.

"No way!"

She checked her mirrors again. Still clear.

She'd passed the last of the businesses a half a block back. Turning this big panel truck around on this narrow street without getting off the pavement wasn't going to be easy but she had to try. She couldn't risk getting stuck in the grass. No snow but damp-looking. Water was puddled here and there.

Rolling her window down, she craned her neck to keep watch. She cut the steering wheel hard to the left, not an easy task. Eased back as far as she dared, then cut hard to the right and eased forward at the same time. Again and again she repeated this maneuver until the truck was facing the opposite direction.

Her arms shook with the effort.

Still no one ran toward her...no vehicle approached.

Where the hell were those guys?

Okay. Now all she had to do was drive past the old warehouse or whatever the huge building was.

If she got up some speed and just kept going no matter what...she'd be okay.

She glanced around the interior of the cab. What she would give for a cell phone just now. Then she surveyed the street.

The men had to be somewhere.

Von tightened her grip on the steering wheel and pressed down on the accelerator.

By the time she reached the building she'd escaped the speedometer read forty-five miles per hour, which was damned fast on this narrow, potholed street.

Relief melted her spine when no shots were fired and no one ran after her.

No orange-and-white-stripped signs for as far as she could see.

"Good to go."

She didn't bother slowing down. If she got picked up on traffic radar that was all the better. The next best thing to having a cell phone right now would be having a cop blue light her.

A black dot appeared in the side mirror.

Von blinked, looked again to make sure she wasn't seeing things.

It was a vehicle.

"No!"

She pressed harder on the accelerator.

How much farther to a populated street?

The approaching vehicle suddenly charged past her.

Her foot eased off the accelerator.

What if that SUV wasn't about her and the children? Could be someone from one of the closed businesses or from some street she didn't know how to get to. It didn't have to be trouble for her.

Her pulse skittered with the burn of adrenaline.

She knew better. This was trouble.

At the end of the block the vehicle skidded to a sideways stop in the road, cutting off her path.

Oh, yeah.

Von hit the brake. The driver's door of the SUV opened. She rammed into Reverse and charged backward, watching her side mirrors but doing a poor job of staying in one lane. The truck swerved.

The SUV straightened and came after her.

The idea that she would pass that building again had a lump of worry clogging her throat.

There was no choice. She had to keep going.

But the street ended.

Panic swelled that lump in her throat.

There was nowhere else to go.

She slammed on the brake.

The truck came to a screeching, jarring stop.

She grimaced when she thought of the girls.

Something hit her foot.

Von looked down. A handgun lay at her feet.

She stretched, reached the weapon.

With her feet on the brake, she grasped the weapon in both hands and braced it on the steering wheel. She closed one eye and zeroed in with the other on the vehicle heading toward her.

Just let them come after her.

Whoever climbed out of that vehicle and started toward the truck…was dead.

Chapter Seventeen

Colby Agency, Chicago, 12:30 p.m. (23 hours missing)

Simon and Ian entered Victoria's office. Simon, in deep conversation on his cell, remained near the door.

She and Jim had been waiting for word...any word on Trinity or Von...and the children.

Since Lane's revelation, Simon had contacted the local Bureau field office. Simon still had difficulty believing that White was on the take. The two had known each other for years.

Ian was working the DA end of things. Lane had been turned over to Chicago PD's custody just over an hour ago.

"District Attorney Brian Ford just called," Ian announced. "Lane lawyered up and isn't talking. He refuses to relate any additional details regarding the drop-off or transfer location without the guarantee of immunity."

Victoria shook her head. "He, of all people, is very much aware of the shortness of time."

"He is. We know," Ian explained, "based on our GPS system that Barrett is in Huntsville, Alabama. As of five minutes ago he was still moving so we don't as of yet have a location of where the next pick-up occurs."

"That's where the good news ends," Simon cut in as he stepped toward Victoria's desk. "At ten-forty-five this morning Agent White's body was discovered in the men's room of a fueling station just off Interchange 565. He was shot point-blank."

"Dear God." Victoria put a hand to her chest. "Nothing on Trinity or Robinson?"

"Nothing," Simon confirmed. "But it gets worse."

"What else?" Jim asked.

Victoria's son looked exhausted. He'd had little sleep. None of them had had more than cat naps. And the situation continued to escalate out of control.

"Since White was with Barrett and Robinson," Simon explained, "APBs have been issued for both."

"If they're detained," Ian went on, "there's no way to know what will become of Von or the children. Not only is their safety still unknown and at risk, there is the issue of the second stream of cargo Lane spoke of. There is no way to get anyone in place to intercede if Barrett and Robinson are in custody."

"It's all happening in the next few hours," Victoria

said, her mind racing to come up with some feasible solution.

"There's nothing law enforcement or the Bureau in Huntsville can do since we don't have a location for the trafficking transaction." Simon shook his head. "If we give them Barrett's location then he'll be taken into custody. And we can't be sure of Robinson's status at this point."

"Our hands are tied until we hear something from Barrett," Jim suggested, uncharacteristic defeat in his tone.

Victoria was having none of that. They were all exhausted, but the Colby Agency never gave up. "Simon, if you can persuade a contact at the Bureau to go with you to Huntsville—via the agency jet— the two of you will be there to work the situation and provide backup to Trinity and Von in real time."

Simon chuckled wearily. "I can try. But keep in mind that the last agent who accompanied one of our people on this investigation was murdered."

"I'll go as well," Ian offered. "Simon will need to work the politics of this delicate situation. I can handle the operational logistics."

Jim stood. "No, I'll go. I should have seen through Lane hours before he made his declaration. It's my shortcoming. I'll make it right."

Victoria held her hands up surrender style. "You gentlemen make the decision. We want Trinity, Von and those children safety returned to us. Lily's mother is conscious and well on her way to recovery, but she needs to hear good news. I have complete faith that the three of you will get the job done."

If it wasn't too late already.

Mildred, Victoria's longtime personal assistant, appeared at her door. "Trinity called. He's discovered the location where Von and the children are supposed to be. Robinson is still cooperating. That's all he had time to tell me."

Victoria felt the first smile in several days. Hope bloomed despite everything. Trinity was alive.

Chapter Eighteen

Von snugged her finger around the trigger as the driver's side door opened.

She wasn't going to let these bastards get their hands on these kids again.

A man emerged from the SUV.

Von blinked.

Trinity.

An audible ache burst from her throat.

She rammed the gearshift into Park and scrambled out of the truck.

They collided in the street between the vehicles.

He hugged her so tightly she couldn't breathe and she didn't care.

He was alive.

When she drew back at last she pounded him on the shoulder. "What took you so damned long?"

"There's a lot we need to talk about," he said, "but right now we have to get off the street." He glanced around as if he feared someone might be watching. "Are the kids okay?"

The kids. She'd probably turned them upside down

and every other way. "Unless my reckless driving caused any injuries."

"We'll check on them as soon as we're out of sight. Drive back to the mill warehouse. We'll take cover there for the moment."

Before she could ask him if he'd lost his mind, he explained, "I neutralized any threat there."

Von couldn't remember ever feeling so relieved. She waited until Trinity turned his vehicle around and then she followed in the truck.

Despite knowing he had neutralized the two goons, anticipation burned in her veins as they approached the old mill warehouse.

Trinity drove his vehicle into the building, she did the same.

They'd made a hell of a lot of noise, couple of gunshots, shattering windshield, bursting through those doors.

But there was apparently no one around to hear.

"Let's check on the kids," Trinity said as soon as Von had climbed out of the truck.

She followed him around to the back and they opened up the truck. It worried her that she hadn't heard any wailing or crying out of her name from back there.

Von showed him how the hidden door in the faux stacked furniture operated. The light from the open doors shone into the back of the truck.

Tousled heads and wide eyes stared out.

Von smiled. "Come on, girls. You don't have to be afraid now."

One by one, the twelve children climbed out of the truck with Tara and Von assisting.

They all veered clear of Trinity until Von explained that he was their friend.

Von had never in her whole life been so happy to see anyone as she was to see Trinity.

If nothing else ever went right in her life again, this would be enough.

"There's a long-wheel base panel van hidden over here," Trinity explained once the little girls were unloaded and reassured.

Using the flashlights the kidnappers had dropped, he directed Von to the far corner of the building where the van was parked and covered. He pulled the drape from the vehicle, revealing the advertisement painted on the side. Premier Roadside Assistance.

Von turned back to look at the truck she'd ridden in across country. "With trying to escape I hadn't noticed that." She gestured to the advertisement painted on it. Southern Family Movers.

"We need to get the girls loaded into the van," Trinity said, drawing her attention back to him. "We have to contact the agency, but first and foremost we have to get out of here so nothing looks amiss."

"You're going to have to explain what exactly is going on," Von said as they moved back to where the girls were huddled.

"Load the girls," he said, "then I'll explain." He

gave her a look that said we can't talk about it in front of the children.

While Von loaded the girls, Trinity moved his SUV to another dark recess of the building. Then, he got the two scumbags who'd driven Von and the girls here and loaded them into the back of the truck. They grunted and groaned, but the tape on their mouths prevented them from saying anything. Once they were in the truck, he taped their ankles together and reinforced the bonds around their wrists.

Trinity went to his SUV and ensured the weapon Robinson had used to murder White was secured. Then he dragged Robinson to the truck to join his colleagues. Once he was secured, Trinity closed them up in the back of the truck just as they had done Von and those sweet little children.

He took the truck keys from the ignition and pocketed them and checked for any other telltale evidence of a scuffle he might have missed.

The drive-through doors were a different story. He wasn't sure what he could do for them after Von's great escape, but he had to try.

When Von had pulled the panel van out of the building, Trinity closed the damaged doors as best he could. They looked like hell but they would have to do.

When he climbed into the passenger seat of the van, Von asked, "What're we doing now?"

Trinity glanced back at the girls seated around

the cargo bay. "We're going to lay low until this is over."

"What about the others?"

"I'll explain—" he nodded toward the kids "—later."

"Where to?"

"Someplace safe."

2:40 p.m.

THE DRIVE TO MONTE SANO MOUNTAIN took twenty minutes. Mildred had relayed that Victoria had personally seen to the arrangements. A three-bedroom cabin, deep in the woods, high atop a mountain.

Bliss, considering what these children had been through. Not to mention Von.

She had spoken to Victoria en route and passed along the girls' names and the names of their parents as well as their addresses. It was a shame to have to keep the girls from the reunion with their parents even for another minute. But until this thing played out, it was the only way to intercept the other children who had been abducted. Robinson had insisted, as had Lane, that more children would be brought to this location for transfer to New Orleans.

Trinity didn't like using one of the scumbag's phones, but it was necessary for the moment. He couldn't risk turning it off and removing the battery in the event there was contact related to the next phase of the operation. He'd contacted the agency as soon as he'd taken it back at the mill warehouse, but only for long enough to relay that he was alive and on track.

"This is it." Trinity turned back to the girls. "We'll be safe here for a while until we can get you home to your families."

Small smiles and weak cheers were his response. The kids were tired and hungry and likely still a little terrified that they would never see their families again. He'd have to find a way to take their minds off those horrors for a little while.

The key was under the mat just as Victoria had said it would be.

Once the girls were inside exploring, Trinity ushered Von to the kitchen and gave her an update.

"Robinson murdered Agent White right in front of you? Are you serious?" she asked, her expression cluttered with disbelief.

Trinity nodded. "These people are ruthless."

Von shook her head and started searching through cabinets for food. Unfortunately the supplies were limited to the essentials. Bare essentials.

"One of the men who drove the truck you were in received a text message that the additional cargo would be delayed. Midnight. With a tentative departure from here immediately thereafter. We have to stay put until midnight at the very least. Or risk losing out on recovering those children."

Von turned to face him and leaned against the

counter. "If anything at all feels off, they could hurt those kids." She shrugged. "Or just keep going."

"Exactly."

"Not to mention you have to stay out of sight," Von reminded him. "It'll take time to get that part straightened out. Until then, you're a wanted man. And I need you."

"I know." Trinity wasn't about to waste time feeling sorry for himself on that count. These were the risks that went with the job. Robinson likely wouldn't confess what he'd done but truth was on Trinity's side. As Von said, it would take time, but justice would prevail.

Besides, he had the Colby Agency on his side.

"Okay, look." Von pushed away from the cabinets. "We need food. And clothes." She looked Trinity straight in the eye. "I'm going shopping. You keep the girls occupied until I get back."

Trinity held up both hands stop-sign fashion. "Whoa. I don't think that's a good idea."

Von braced her hands on her hips. "I'm not the one with the APB sporting my description. I'll be fine. There was a supercenter in the valley right before we started up the mountain. I'll be back in less than an hour."

There was no arguing with Von Cassidy when she made up her mind. Trinity gave her the cash he'd brought with him and the agency credit card.

And she was off.

He strolled into the great room where the girls were piled around the television.

So long as no one was bleeding or crying, he was happy.

THE SUPERCENTER WAS PACKED.

Christmas stuff was everywhere.

Von was always relieved when the holiday was over.

Those last-minute shoppers just wouldn't give up until the bitter end.

Von shook her head as she guided her cart through the masses of bodies. Didn't people have better things to do?

Since she wasn't exactly sure of the girls' sizes, she'd selected stretchy sweat shirts and sweat pants in children's smalls and mediums and a couple of larges and in a variety of colors. Undies. And a pink set of the same in her size. A new shirt for Trinity.

Pizza. Lots of pizza and chips and soft drinks.

Cookies, and more cookies.

After what these kids had been through, they deserved all the junk food they wanted.

Since she didn't want to use the cash or answer any questions and show ID, Von used the self-checkout line. It took a little longer, but she managed.

Once she'd swiped the credit card and signed off, she was ready to bag her goods and get out of this zoo.

If she hadn't plopped a bag in the cart at just that

moment or hadn't glanced at the Santa for charity bell ringer outside the entrance doors, she wouldn't have seen her.

But she did.

The blonde…the one Von had seen back at the barn transfer location in Chicago.

She was outside the store speaking on her cell phone. A big, broad-shouldered man stood close by.

Could be coincidence.

Huntsville was a fair-sized town, but still small compared to Chicago.

Von loaded her purchases into her cart and pretended to check the bags one last time. With her head down, she scanned the front of the store to see what the blonde would do next.

The man with her headed back out to the parking lot, his cell phone pressed to his ear.

Von's heart seemed to stop beating as she watched the man walk directly to the slot where she'd parked the van. He circled it, all the while in deep conversation on his cell.

They had tracked the van here.

Something else she should have thought of.

The blonde entered the store and surveyed the crowd.

Von bent forward and tucked a bag on the bottom rack of the cart.

She had to get out of here, had to call Trinity.

There was no back way out of the supercenter. Only the main entrance and exit at the front.

Von was going to have to get creative.

She left her cart near the video rental kiosk and walked to the ladies room.

Inside, she checked the stalls to ensure all were vacant.

She pulled the cell phone Trinity had insisted she take with her from her pocket and called the cabin. There was no way to know for certain if they had tracked her here using the van or the phone, but this call had to be made.

"Hello."

Trinity didn't identify himself but Von knew his voice as well as she knew her own. "Get the children out of there now."

"What's going on, Von?"

"They've tracked the van or the cell." She shook her head. "I don't know. But if they know I'm in this store, they know I've been at the cabin. Get them out." She tried to think what they'd passed on the road to the cabin. "The church," she blurted. "There was a church a mile or so from there. Walk them through the woods until you reach the church."

"Von," Trinity said when she would have ended the call.

"Yeah?"

"What're you going to do?"

She laughed softly. "You know me. I always figure something out. See you in a bit." She closed the phone before he could say anything else. On her way out the restroom door she dropped it into the trash bin.

Strangely her cart still sat by the exit when she moved in that direction. The blonde was obviously combing the store searching for Von.

Right now, Von needed a ride.

Since the guy who'd been hanging around the blonde hadn't looked familiar to Von, she was going to assume they had never met.

Because he was still outside, loitering around the van.

Von pushed her cart alongside a man's who was exiting at the same time.

"Looks like another Christmas without snow," she commented with a big smile. She had no idea what else to chat about. She wasn't one to keep up with sports and she knew absolutely nothing about hunting.

"If you live here long enough," the man said with an answering smile, "you get used to that."

Keeping a wary eye on the man near the van, Von just keep walking right alongside her new friend. He was regaling her with the advantages of being a schoolteacher and having the holidays off. She was nodding and making agreeable sounds.

They could have been any other couple in town.

"Have a merry Christmas," he said as he stopped at the trunk of what was presumably his car.

"You, too!" Von called, moving two cars over.

While he loaded his goods, she searched her pockets. "Oh, no!"

The man looked up from closing his trunk.

"I've locked my keys in my car." She held her hands palms up.

He pushed his cart aside and started in her direction. "Is there anything I can do?"

She hurried away from the car with her own cart in tow. "I've done this before. My husband's going to kill me. I guess I'll have to call him to come get me."

"That's a shame." The man shook his head.

"He'll have to drag the twins out," she said when her last comment didn't do it.

"Twins?"

She nodded. "Only three months old."

His face puckered with concern. "Well I'd hate for him to have to do that. You live nearby?"

"Just up the road."

"Fine," he offered with a nod. "I'll give you a ride then. It's practically Christmas but it's the neighborly thing to do in any season."

With her purchases loaded, Von sank into the seat and relaxed as he pulled out of the supercenter parking lot.

Her nerves were shot.

Any more close calls like this and she was going to have to think about changing careers.

Her Good Samaritan looked at her a little strangely

when Von told him she lived in the house behind the church.

"Reverend Hardin's house?"

Not good. He knew the place. "Yes. He's my uncle. My husband and I are staying there until we find our own place. We just moved down from Chicago. He was transferred with his job. Are you a member of my uncle's church?"

The driver shook his head. "I should be, I suppose." He flashed a smile. "Not much of a churchgoer."

Von had to bite her tongue.

He offered to help with the bags, but she insisted he hurry on home. His family was probably waiting. It was almost Christmas Eve, after all.

When he'd driven away, Von stood there surrounded by blue plastic bags.

The cold whipped around her and she felt ready to collapse. It was getting dark, this day was almost over. But the battle was just beginning.

Since there hadn't been anyone at the front of the church, she walked around to the back. No one outside but there was a door that appeared to lead into the back of the church or more accurately a closed in porch of sorts. Von opened the door and stepped inside. A long, narrow room, the walls lined with windows and benches, the benches lined with little girls. Trinity turned toward Von and their gazes locked.

"You okay?"

She nodded. She was tired. Emotion welled in her throat. She was so glad he was here.

Trinity walked over and tilted her chin up to get a better look at her face and the breakdown she was trying really hard to hide. "Don't worry," he said softly. "We're safe and that's all that matters."

She nodded jerkily. What he said was right. She knew. She was just too tired to cope at the moment.

"Come." He ushered her over to a bench to sit next to the girls. "Stay put. I'll figure this out."

Chapter Nineteen

4:51 p.m.

Trinity approached the house behind the church. There were no lights on inside and one vehicle parked in the drive, a minivan.

Could be someone home despite the lack of lights as night approached.

The house was likely the church parsonage and it was almost Christmas Eve. Surely if there was someone home they wouldn't turn away twelve little girls.

Silent inside. Trinity knocked on the door. Still quiet. The occasional vehicle passing on the street in front of the church was the only sound.

A couple more knocks and he felt convinced that no one was home.

He checked under the welcome mat, then the little concrete angel sitting near the door. The house key was under the angel.

People in the south could usually be counted on for leaving a house key handy.

There were no signs announcing one security system or the other protected the house. Trinity hoped he wasn't about to alert the police to his location.

No beeps, whistles or bells sounded when he opened the door. He felt on the wall for a light switch and turned on the overhead fixture. The lack of a keypad near the door signaled that a security system was not part of the home's amenities.

Trinity walked through the house, from the kitchen through the three bedrooms and home office. No sign of anyone. Most telling was that there was no milk in the refrigerator and no gifts under the Christmas tree. Kids lived here and the absence of milk and gifts was a good sign that the family wasn't home and wouldn't be back for a few days.

Headed for the door to go after Von and the kids, the telephone rang, stopping Trinity in his tracks. On the third ring the answering machine was activated.

Hello, you've reached the Hardin family. Be back for services Christmas Eve night. Leave us a message or call our cell phone. God bless.

They had the house for the night.

Some of Trinity's tension eased. He hurried back to the church. They could all use a few hours of un-guarded relaxation.

He opened the back door of the church and stuck his head inside. "Come on. We have a place for the night." He grinned. "The preacher and his family are away until tomorrow."

Von released a big puff of air. "Great." She stood. "Come on, girls."

Trinity held the door as the girls marched out. He had to smile as he watched Von leading the troop toward the parsonage.

And she'd thought she wouldn't make a good mother after losing the baby.

Trinity shook his head. She would make a great mother.

Von supervised a dozen showers while Trinity prepared pizza. Lots of pizza. And green beans. Kids needed something green with each meal, his mother had always insisted. With no salad fixings available, he'd opened the three cans of green beans he found in the cupboard. He doubted the girls would be overjoyed, but at least the beans were green.

There was no milk in the house but there were fruit drinks. While the oven took care of dinner, Trinity put in a call to the agency. Victoria needed to be aware of this latest turn of events.

The news from her end was not encouraging.

By the time the pizzas were sliced and the green beans in a serving bowl on the counter, twelve little angels appeared, each dressed in new sweats. Pinks, blues and greens.

The Hardins had paper plates and disposable cups

which would make for easier clean up. Trinity passed around a roll of paper towels for napkins.

Stretched out on the floor in front of the television, the girls gobbled down their pizza and picked at their beans. Trinity brought Von up to speed while they consumed their equally appetizing dinner.

"Victoria, along with the Bureau liaison, are contacting all the girls' parents to let them know their children are safe and will be home by tomorrow."

"I'm certain there are some relieved parents in the Chicago area tonight. Wow." Von cast a lingering glance at the girls. "The idea that these children could have been lost forever…" She visibly shuddered. "It's just unthinkable." She met Trinity's eyes. "I talked to each of the girls and none seems to have been harmed in any way, other than being mentally terrorized. I didn't see any indication of physical abuse. No bruises or scrapes of any kind."

"Thank God," Trinity said, his heart relieved. "There's more," he went on with his update. "Robinson and the others are dead." He imagined Von wouldn't suffer any regrets over that aspect of this horrific business.

She shook her head. "That's a shame but it's hard to feel any sympathy for guys like that." She met Trinity's gaze. "So whoever's running this operation knows."

Trinity nodded. "Some homeless people seeking shelter went into the old mill warehouse and discovered the bodies. The moving truck and the SUV were still inside. The local authorities are hounding Victoria as to my whereabouts."

Von rubbed her forehead. "This just gets worse and worse."

"Jim, Ian and Simon, along with some other agent from the Bureau are here."

That surprised Von. "In Huntsville?"

"Landed maybe an hour ago. They're trying to straighten out this mess with the local authorities. We're to stay put until morning. Victoria said the mill warehouse is under surveillance, but I don't think that'll help at this point."

"Definitely not." Von picked up the paper plate and tossed the remains of her dinner into the trash. She turned back to Trinity. "They know their rendezvous location here has been compromised, as have their operatives who they obviously terminated. Their cargo is missing and the plan for getting these kids to New Orleans is dead in the water. I just hope someone can find the other kids that were supposed to be picked up here."

"It would make sense," Trinity said, the idea jelling in his head, "that if the bad guys are still trying to track us down…then everything's at a standstill."

"Possibly," Von agreed. "The blonde." She plowed her fingers through her hair. "I know that blonde girl from somewhere. She was with the man in charge. He wore the kind of suit you don't find on the racks at department stores."

Trinity surveyed the girls scattered on the living

room floor. "I know this is a big financial loss to him and his operation, but why risk getting caught over one lost shipment? This operation is too well executed, too sophisticated to take that kind of risk."

Von braced her hands on the counter and considered his words. "Maybe," she said, "this guy just doesn't like to lose." She met Trinity's gaze. "He was going to auction me for those deadly fight matches."

Trinity's gut twisted at the idea. "The agency needs to stop that bastard." The idea that White had been an insider outraged Trinity all over again.

"Why don't you take a shower first?" Von suggested. "I'll get the girls settled and then," she grinned, "I'm going to have a long soak in that big tub I saw in the master bathroom."

Trinity tried to suppress the images her words prompted. Didn't work. "Sounds good to me."

He hesitated before going for that shower. "Thanks for the shirt, by the way."

"There are toiletries and…ah…underwear, too." Her cheeks pinked.

He had to grin. "Are you blushing?"

She shook her head. "Absolutely not! I got what we all needed. It's no big deal."

"Uh-huh."

"Just go, Barrett," she scolded firmly, but the laugh that followed was genuine.

It was good to hear her laugh.

It had been way too long.

* * *

7:05 p.m.

"MY TURN." VON GAVE Trinity a high five as she passed him in the hallway outside the bedrooms. "The girls are down for the count." It was early but they were all exhausted and well fed for the first time in at least a couple of days.

Von turned, moving backward very slowly, to watch Trinity walk away. He looked really good in that white shirt and the jeans. His feet were bare and his hair was still a little damp.

She smiled when he stopped at the first bedroom door. He stood there a moment, then moved on to the next one. Von had tucked the girls into the queen-sized beds, six to a room. With three girls at the head and three at the foot of each bed, it worked out nicely. Except for the pillow situation. She'd had a heck of a time tracking down enough pillows. Leaving a bedside lamp on to keep the darkness at bay had satisfied the children.

Each one had insisted on a good-night kiss. Von shook her head. She never made it a habit of kissing children. Tonight she'd kissed twelve, one right after the other. Her chest tightened. They were safe…for now.

How could a person have a child and ever let them out of their sight?

Von didn't see how parents did it.

The worry…the sheer terror…of just dropping them off at school.

Maybe that was why she'd lost the baby. Maybe she wasn't cut out for being a parent.

Okay, she needed a bath. A long, hot bath.

The master bathroom was a little small but there was a nice-sized tub. That was all Von needed. She started the water running and then dug around under the sink for soaking oils or bubble bath. Anything to cleanse away the stench of scumbags.

"Aha!" It wasn't a luxurious soaking oil but it was a nicely scented bubble bath that promised to relax her muscles. Von poured a couple of capfuls into the bath water and rounded up two towels.

She started to slip off her clothes, then remembered the sweats and undies she'd bought for herself. Back in the bedroom she snagged the bag and closed herself in the bathroom once more.

Leaving her two-day-old attire on the tile floor, she sank into the wonderfully warm water and relaxed.

It felt so good.

So, so, so good.

She closed her eyes and allowed her muscles to relax.

Slowly the insanity of the past twenty-four hours dissolved.

Somewhere on the fringes of sleep, images whispered through her mind. Trinity touching her…his lips moving over her body. Her body shivered. *I love you…*

Von's eyes snapped open. She sat up. Shivered. The water had cooled.

She climbed out, drained and rinsed the tub, then slowly dried her body. Her skin was sensitive to her own touch. Her insides still quivering from the dreams of Trinity touching her.

When she'd discarded her old clothes—which she never wanted to see again—into the store bag, she dressed in the new items she'd purchased.

The house was quiet as she made her way down the hall. The girls were all sleeping soundly. *Good.* She put her bag of trashed clothes next to the others, the girls' discarded clothes and the dinner trash, then she frowned. The sofa now blocked the front door. Good move, but...

Where was Trinity?

She wandered into the kitchen. The two rooms were open to each other, divided by a long bar. She was halfway across the big kitchen when the back door opened.

Von jumped, put her hand over her mouth but not quickly enough to stifle the gasp.

"Sorry." Trinity tinkered with the door, then pushed it closed and locked it. He slid a cabinet, kind of like a small china cabinet, in front of the back door. "Just taking a few precautions."

He was worried that whoever had killed Robinson and his cronies would still come after the kids...and the two people responsible for rescuing them.

Shouldering out of his coat, he gifted her with a

reassuring smile. "Don't worry. We're going to be fine."

The weapon in the waistband of his jeans reminded her that they were armed. She'd tucked the weapon he gave her under the mattress in the master bedroom.

"I know." She shivered in spite of her assertion. "I'm just tired."

He tossed his coat onto the bar. "Come on." He draped an arm around her shoulders. "You need sleep." He ushered her down the hall to the bedroom.

She stood there, staring at him as he drew the covers back. He was right. She understood that. But she didn't want to be alone.

"I'll take the couch," he said. "Victoria has the number here. If there are any developments she'll contact us. Otherwise we're to stay put until we receive new orders."

All true. And him sleeping on the couch was a good idea. She completely agreed.

But it wasn't what she wanted him to do at this moment.

She looked up at him, wondered why on earth she hadn't recognized what a mistake she'd made five years ago before now. It hadn't been his fault they'd lost the baby. That he'd wanted to try again, later when they were older and more financially secure, had been smart. But she'd been too damaged to be reasonable. She'd lost everything that ever mattered to her. Her parents…her baby… She couldn't bear to have him die on her, too. So she'd made him go. She'd forced him out of her life…so she couldn't lose him that way.

She'd been crazy with hurt…too young to cope.

Was it too late to fix that now?

"I want you here…" She moistened her lips, mostly to buy time and to shore up her courage. "With me."

Trinity didn't question her. Didn't argue. He closed the door softly, turned the knob to lock it. Then he reached for her.

His boots and their clothes landed in a pile on the floor. When her body was skin-to-skin with his she felt as if she were home for the first time in five years.

He lowered her to the bed, his lips working that magic that only Trinity Barrett could work on her. Despite the urgency she felt in his body, he took his time. He lavished every part of her with attention until she felt ready to scream with need. She bit her lips together, didn't want to wake the girls…didn't want anything but him touching her like this…forever.

When he sank into her…she was complete.

Time stopped and there was nothing but his touch…his soft whispers…and the incredible sensation of ecstasy.

TRINITY'S ENTIRE BODY shuddered with the climax that only Von could bring in him. He'd wanted no

other woman except her. She was his soul mate…
his wife no matter that legal documents indicated
otherwise.

She was his…there would never be anyone else.

He held her close, was terrified by the prospect of
letting go.

Von kissed his chest. "When this is over," she
murmured, "we're going to have that talk you've been
asking about."

A smile tugged at his lips even as emotion burned
his eyes. "'Bout time," he whispered.

She nodded, her cheek caressing his skin.
"Definitely."

He kissed the top of her head, relished the feel of
her silky hair. "Sleep. I'll keep watch."

As badly as he hated to, he untangled himself from
her sweet, warm body and pulled on his clothes and
boots.

He gathered her clothes and placed them on the
bed before kissing her cheek. "Just in case." He patted
her clothes.

They had to be prepared…just in case.

Thursday, December 24th, 12:03 a.m.

VON HEARD A BELL.

She sat up. Blinked.

"Put the girls under the beds."

Her gaze flew to Trinity's. He pressed a finger to

his lips before she could ask the question on the tip of her tongue, then he disappeared down the hall.

Trouble was here.

Von reached under the mattress and got the weapon she'd stashed there. Staying low, she crept into the first bedroom and awakened Tara.

"Shh." She put her fingers against the girl's mouth. "Quiet. I need all of you under the bed. Now."

Tara nodded, her eyes still cluttered with sleep.

It took a full minute, but Von and Tara finally got the girls under the bed.

Von moved on to the next room.

This time it wasn't so easy.

There were plaster containers of toys stashed under the bed. Von pushed the containers into the closet while April helped the others get under the bed.

Something crashed in the kitchen.

The cabinet, she realized.

Damn.

Gunshots shattered the silence.

Cries echoed from beneath the bed.

Von hunkered down next to the bed. "Stay quiet," she whispered. "And don't move."

She crawled to the door, checked the hall and then hurried to the next bedroom. More sobbing. She moved close to the bed and grabbed Tara's hand. "We'll be okay. But we have to stay very still and very quiet."

Tara nodded.

The sobbing stopped but another crash echoed from the living room-kitchen area.

Maintaining a crouch, Von moved in that direction, her weapon palmed and ready.

Trinity had one man down and was taking on a second.

Von eased closer, not daring to stand and make herself a target in front of the many windows.

The man was working hard to pull the muzzle of his weapon down to Trinity's face. Trinity was working equally hard to keep it away.

Von lowered onto her belly and braced her elbows on the floor. She took aim…held her breath…and fired.

The bastard's knee buckled as the bullet passed through his thigh.

A scream rent the air. He released his weapon and crumpled to the floor, curling into a ball of agony.

Trinity snatched up the dropped weapon and shouted to her, "Get back! There's more of them out there."

A window crashed and something tumbled onto the floor.

Canister.

"Gas!" Trinity shouted at the same instant Von recognized the danger.

She jumped to her feet and rushed back into the hall. "Don't come out," she shouted to the girls as she slammed the first bedroom door. She dove into the second bedroom and shoved the door shut.

"What's happening?" Tara poked her head from under the bed.

"Stay under the bed," Von urged. She wanted to open the windows but that would only announce their exact location to the enemy.

Instead, she slowed her breathing and tried not to inhale the fumes leaking under the door.

"Don't be afraid," Von whispered, her head already spinning. "It's Christmas Eve…"

Nothing bad could happen…not today.

Chapter Twenty

Von wasn't sitting in this damned room another second.

She hopped off the exam table and walked out in the not-so-attractive hospital gown. Who cared?

Jim Colby, obviously deep in conversation with two men Von didn't recognize, turned toward her. "There's one of our heroes." Jim waved her over. "Let me introduce you to Special Agent in Charge Vince Latham and his deputy, Special Agent Melvin Wells. They represent the Huntsville field office."

Von shook hands. "Thank you." She wondered which of them had given the order to gas the parsonage. At the time, no one had known how many of the enemy was inside…seemed like the thing to do if anyone was going to be saved when backup showed up on the scene.

Thankfully Jim and Ian had been close by, just waiting for the enemy to show.

"Thank you," Latham insisted. "You and Mr. Barrett saved those children."

"What about the others?" Von turned to Jim. "There was supposed to be another pickup here."

"One of the men captured this morning broke at two-thirty," Jim assured her. "Four other children were recovered and are here as well."

"Are they okay?" Von's heart bumped into a faster rhythm.

"They're fine. Like the others, the examinations were merely a precaution."

Von still had a bit of a headache from the sleeping gas. "Where's Trinity?"

Jim pointed to the room next to the one Von had exited. "The doctor's still with him, but he should be out soon."

Von nodded. "The kids?"

"I'll show you," Wells spoke up.

Jim gave her a final pat on the shoulder before she followed the agent down the wide corridor. They passed several treatment rooms, but he didn't stop until they reached the last door.

Inside was one big treatment room with several beds. Numerous gurneys had been pulled into the room to facilitate the girls.

"They wanted to be together," Wells explained.

"Miss Von!"

Von lost count of the times she was hugged. The girls' sweats had been exchanged for little hospital gowns printed with cartoon characters and animals. Not nearly so ugly as the one Von wore.

The best part was that they were all fine.

Just fine.

"Their parents should be arriving from the airport any minute now," Wells told her when the girls had wandered back to the coloring books and crayons provided by the staff.

"Wow." Von was surprised. "That's fast."

"This Victoria Colby-Camp person is something," Wells said with admiration. "She, apparently, got on the phone with some of the rich folks she knows in Chicago. Three private planes were scrambled within the hour to bring the parents of all twelve children here." He shrugged. "It is Christmas Eve, you know."

"It is," Von said, tears welling in her eyes despite her best efforts to hold them back.

Before she could tell the girls she would be back in a bit, the door opened and people crowded in.

Not just people, she realized, the *parents*. The last to enter was Wanda Larkin, wheelchair-bound but here nonetheless. Jolie Ruhl, Simon's wife, pushed the wheelchair. She flashed a smile at Von.

Von and Wells stepped back and watched the incredible reunion. It was the most remarkable thing Von had ever witnessed.

It was truly a Christmas miracle.

This, Von admitted, was what Christmas was really about.

She turned to leave the room, giving the families the privacy they deserved, and Trinity waited in the doorway for her. He wasn't wearing an ugly gown like she was. He had on those rugged jeans and cowboy boots, along with the white shirt she'd bought him.

She rushed into his arms. He hugged her tight.

"Come on, let's find your clothes." He ushered her into the corridor. "We have a debriefing."

"Already?" Von was surprised. "Here?"

He nodded. "It can't wait."

4:40 a.m.

THE HOSPITAL HAD PROVIDED a conference room used by the doctors. Jim Colby, Simon Ruhl, and Ian Michaels were all present. Victoria and the special agent in charge of the Chicago field office had been tied in via a teleconferencing system. Agents Latham and Wells, Madison County Police Chief Chet Crabtree and three other detectives were also included.

"Four men are dead," Latham began. "All a part of the trafficking organization responsible for the abduction of the girls we are pleased to say are all unharmed."

Applause swelled around the room.

"Three of this organization have been taken into custody and are currently being interrogated. Only one has broken his silence and we are most thankful for that since four more children were recovered."

More applause. As exhausted as Von felt, she wanted to jump up and down and cheer. They had won. The children were safe.

Trinity couldn't help himself, he reached for Von's hand under the table. She didn't resist. In fact, she smiled up at him. His heart did some crazy fluttering.

"But," Latham said somberly, "we have some hard work ahead of us. This is only the tip of the iceberg. We believe this organization is one of the largest human trafficking networks in this country. They must be stopped." He looked around the room. "It will take all our combined forces to make that happen. This morning SAIC, Special Agent in Charge, Bream of Chicago and I were authorized to create a special task force including detectives from numerous jurisdictions between Chicago and New Orleans." Like a fire and brimstone preacher, Latham flattened his palms on the table and eyed each person seated for an intense moment. "We will stop this evil."

Von raised her hand, the one Trinity wasn't holding.

Latham pointed to her. "Miss Cassidy." He gestured to the room at large. "I believe everyone here is aware that Miss Cassidy and her colleague, Mr. Barrett, were pivotal in this significant break."

The applause was deafening this time. Trinity gave a nod of acknowledgement.

"You have something to share, Miss Cassidy," Latham said when the applause had diminished.

"While I was being held in the Chicago location," Von began, "and then again here in Huntsville, I saw a young woman I'm certain I recognized."

Utter silence fell over the assembled group.

"Blonde, maybe twenty-three or -four." Von shook her head. "I'm convinced she was an abduction victim about six years back. It was highly publicized. All over the news for months. She was on a high school graduation trip. Her name was Tina...or Terri." Von shook her head in frustration. "Something like that."

"Tessa Woods," one of the detectives said. "From Purvis, Mississippi."

"That's her." Von nodded, sat up straighter. "I'm nearly certain it was her."

Latham turned to his deputy. "Wells, get us a photo of Miss Woods."

The debrief continued from there with an underlying anticipation that throbbed with hope. When the photo of Tessa Woods was sent to Agent Wells's phone, Von confirmed that the woman she had seen working with these bastards was indeed Tessa Woods or, at least, a woman who looked exactly like her.

When the meeting concluded, Trinity and Von followed Jim and the other Colby folks into the corridor.

"We're finished here," Jim said. "The agency jet is prepared for takeoff. Jolie, Wanda and Lily Larkin, will be flying back to Chicago with us. The other parents and children have transportation at their disposal to do the same. What about you two? Are you ready to return or do you need a few days to decompress?"

"Excuse me," Simon interrupted with a wave of his cell phone before stepping away.

Trinity turned to Von. "You need a vacation?"

She exhaled. "Definitely."

Simon approached the huddle. "Pardon me again," he said, looking first at Trinity and then Von, "Victoria would like to speak to the two of you privately." He passed the phone to Trinity. "You can use the conference room since it's clear now." He smiled. "Put the phone on speaker."

Trinity and Von exchanged a look of confusion.

"Don't worry," Jim said knowingly, "we'll wait."

Inside the conference room, Trinity pressed the speaker button on the phone and placed it on the conference table. "Yes, Victoria. Von and I are both here."

"I think the two of you need some time off," Victoria said, cutting straight to the chase. "I've taken the liberty, with Mildred's help, of reserving a lovely mountain retreat for the two of you in Gatlinburg. It's only a few hours' drive from Huntsville. They tell me the snow is lovely just now."

Judging by the look on Von's face she didn't know what to say any more than Trinity did. "That's not necessary, Victoria. We…" We what? He wanted to do this more than words could convey…but did Von? He looked to her and shrugged.

"We…know we have final reports to turn in," Von said. "And…" She turned her palms up with the same *I dunno* look.

"Let's not pretend we don't all know the facts," Victoria said pointedly. "Here at the Colby Agency, we know our people. We support our people. You two have a second chance here. Take it."

Trinity smiled. "I do believe that's a direct order."

"It most definitely is," Victoria confirmed.

"Well then," Von said hesitantly, "I guess we'll be taking a vacation."

"There's a rental waiting in the parking lot," Victoria informed them. "Mildred will forward your reservation information to Simon's phone—which you'll be using until you return to Chicago."

Von and Trinity recited, "Yes, ma'am," in unison.

Trinity closed the phone, ending the call. He looked Von up and down. "I think our first order of business is a shopping spree."

Von shook her head. "I hate last-minute shoppers."

Trinity pulled her into his arms. "Or maybe we won't need any clothes."

"I like the way you think, Barrett."

They finalized their negotiations with a kiss.

It was almost Christmas…anything was possible.

Chapter Twenty-One

Chicago, Christmas Day

Victoria watched as her granddaughter opened more presents. She imagined that Lily Larkin was having a similarly happy Christmas. The Colby Agency had showered the Larkin apartment with gifts for both mother and daughter.

The day was perfect. Victoria looked around her son's living room. They were all together. Safe and happy.

As if reading her mind, Lucas pulled her close and kissed her cheek. "I have a special Christmas present for you, darling."

She looked up at him, breathless. He still did that to her, even after all these years. "And what's that?" As if he hadn't already given her the world.

"Day before yesterday I officially retired."

Victoria felt her eyes widen. "What?" That was impossible. Lucas Camp retired?

He nodded. "From now on, I'm working with you

at the Colby Agency." He grinned. "You'll be my only boss."

Then he placed a soft, lingering kiss on her lips.

Clapping and whistling from across the room interrupted their sweet celebration.

"Now there's something worth celebrating," Jim said.

"Hear, hear," Tasha added, baby Luke in her arms.

Victoria blinked back the emotion in her eyes. "This truly is a magical Christmas."

"Jim has news as well," Tasha announced with a nudge of her handsome husband.

"Do tell," Lucas encouraged.

"I'm meeting with a buyer for the brownstone next week," Jim said. "He's interested in purchasing the building and the name, the Equalizers. According to his attorney, he intends to start a similar shop of his own."

"That's great news," Victoria said, very pleased. "You and Tasha can start looking for that country home you've been talking about."

Tasha grinned. "I've already gotten in touch with a Realtor."

Jim and Tasha had been considering purchasing a large country estate. The sale of the brownstone would go a long way in making that purchase. Victoria had offered to buy a property for them, but her son would have no part in it. He was doing this on his own.

That was the Colby in him. Undying determination and fearless independence.

Christmas miracles, Victoria decided. The past few days had been filled with that magic.

Another year was behind them and the Colby legacy continued to thrive.

* * * * *

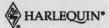

INTRIGUE

COMING NEXT MONTH

Available December 7, 2010

#1245 MAN WITH THE MUSCLE
Bodyguard of the Month
Julie Miller

#1246 WINCHESTER CHRISTMAS WEDDING
Whitehorse, Montana: Winchester Ranch Reloaded
B.J. Daniels

#1247 COLBY CORE
Colby Agency: Christmas Miracles
Debra Webb

#1248 WILD STALLION
Texas Maternity: Labor and Delivery
Delores Fossen

#1249 GENUINE COWBOY
Sons of Troy Ledger
Joanna Wayne

#1250 A SILVERHILL CHRISTMAS
Carol Ericson

REQUEST YOUR FREE BOOKS!

2 FREE NOVELS
PLUS 2
FREE GIFTS!

HARLEQUIN®

INTRIGUE®

Breathtaking Romantic Suspense

HI10R

See below for a sneak peek from our classic
Harlequin® Romance® line.

Introducing DADDY BY CHRISTMAS by Patricia Thayer.

MIA caught sight of Jarrett when he walked into the open lobby. It was hard not to notice the man. In a charcoal business suit with a crisp white shirt and striped tie covered by a dark trench coat, he looked more Wall Street than small-town Colorado.

Mia couldn't blame him for keeping his distance. He was probably tired of taking care of her.

Besides, why would a man like Jarrett McKane be interested in her? Why would he want to take on a woman expecting a baby? Yet he'd done so many things for her. He'd been there when she'd needed him most. How could she not care about a man like that?

Heart pounding in her ears, she walked up behind him. Jarrett turned to face her. "Did you get enough sleep last night?"

"Yes, thanks to you," she said, wondering if he'd thought about their kiss. Her gaze went to his mouth, then she quickly glanced away. "And thank you for not bringing up my meltdown."

Jarrett couldn't stop looking at Mia. Blue was definitely her color, bringing out the richness of her eyes.

"What meltdown?" he said, trying hard to focus on what she was saying. "You were just exhausted from lack of sleep and worried about your baby."

He couldn't help remembering how, during the night, he'd kept going in to watch her sleep. How strange was that? "I hope you got enough rest."

She nodded. "Plenty. And you're a good neighbor for

coming to my rescue."

He tensed. Neighbor? *What neighbor kisses you like I did?* "That's me, just the full-service landlord," he said, trying to keep the sarcasm out of his voice. He started to leave, but she put her hand on his arm.

"Jarrett, what I meant was you went beyond helping me." Her eyes searched his face. "I've asked far too much of you."

"Did you hear me complain?"

She shook her head. "You should. I feel like I've taken advantage."

"Like I said, I haven't minded."

"And I'm grateful for everything…"

Grasping her hand on his arm, Jarrett leaned forward. The memory of last night's kiss had him aching for another. "I didn't do it for your gratitude, Mia."

Gorgeous tycoon Jarrett McKane has never believed in Christmas—but he can't help being drawn to soon-to-be-mom Mia Saunders! Christmases past were spent alone…and now Jarrett may just have a fairy-tale ending for all his Christmases future!

Available December 2010, only from Harlequin® Romance®.